It would solve the
decided with a wi

Struck by a sneaky sp
rocking and sat bolt upright on her perch.

Temptation whispered that even the smallest chance Max would marry her to save her girls enduring a life as an unwanted duty to their grandfather for the next ten or fifteen years was worth a try. A platonic marriage with the one man she could trust not to force his repellent needs on her could get her children away from Edgar's family for good. Did she have enough gall to ask such an impossible thing of an old friend? Yes, for her girls' sake, she would do anything she had to if it meant she could keep them safe.

She hated dragging Max into this mess as well, but if only he would say yes, she could stay at Holdfast for a while, pretend she could not endure the country, and they could live a few hundred miles apart for most of the year. She could spend a few weeks in Northumberland with him every summer, and he could spare one or two every now and again to keep up appearances in London. It was a last desperate throw of the dice, and it probably wouldn't work, but she was still going to try it.

Author Note

Sometimes an idea for a book comes to me after a lot of thinking and hoping and rejecting the wrong ones, and sometimes one just turns up and demands to be written. When Max appeared in my last book, *Secrets of the Viscount's Bride*, to give his brother Zachary someone to talk to before his wedding, I knew Max must have his own story. He watched his brother pace with nerves and impatience to marry his heroine and said, "I am never going to get married." And he was only twenty, so I had to know why.

This is my answer to a question I often get asked: Where do you get your ideas from? Sometimes I have to work hard to find ones that will work, and sometimes they simply drop into my lap. Thank you, Max, for dropping in like that. I have loved working with you and here's hoping that my wonderful readers love you, too!

ELIZABETH BEACON

—

A Proposal to Protect His Lady

HARLEQUIN®
HISTORICAL™

PLEASE RECYCLE · THIS PRODUCT IS RECYCLABLE

Recycling programs
for this product may
not exist in your area.

ISBN-13: 978-1-335-59602-4

A Proposal to Protect His Lady

Copyright © 2024 by Elizabeth Beacon

For questions and comments about the quality of this book, please contact us at CustomerService@Harlequin.com.

TM and ® are trademarks of Harlequin Enterprises ULC.

Harlequin Enterprises ULC
22 Adelaide St. West, 41st Floor
Toronto, Ontario M5H 4E3, Canada
www.Harlequin.com

Printed in U.S.A.

Elizabeth Beacon has a passion for history and storytelling and, with the English West Country on her doorstep, never lacks a glorious setting for her books. Elizabeth tried horticulture, higher education as a mature student, briefly taught English and worked in an office before finally turning her daydreams about dashing piratical heroes and their stubborn, independent heroines into her dream job: writing Regency romances for Harlequin Historical.

Books by Elizabeth Beacon

Harlequin Historical

A Rake to the Rescue
The Duchess's Secret
Falling for the Scandalous Lady
Lady Helena's Secret Husband
Secrets of the Viscount's Bride
A Proposal to Protect His Lady

The Yelverton Marriages

Marrying for Love or Money?
Unsuitable Bride for a Viscount
The Governess's Secret Longing

A Year of Scandal

The Viscount's Frozen Heart
The Marquis's Awakening
Lord Laughraine's Summer Promise
Redemption of the Rake
The Winterley Scandal
The Governess Heiress

Visit the Author Profile page
at Harlequin.com for more titles.

Prologue

January 1810

Waiting in a wood at dawn, Max Chilton shifted from one cold foot to the other and wished he was fighting neglect at Holdfast Castle in Northumberland instead of meeting a woman who had buried her husband yesterday. It was his own fault. If he hadn't gone to Mynham after the funeral to catch a glimpse of the widow, she could not have slipped him a note saying to meet her at this godforsaken hour.

Georgia had stolen his heart when they were both eighteen and three years on he wasn't sure he had got it back yet. His childhood partner in mischief had turned into a luminously beautiful young woman between one day and the next and watched him with puzzled eyes whenever he tried to court her in such a clumsy, tongue-tied way that he almost blushed when he thought about it even now. Then she went to London to make her debut in polite society and he followed her like a devoted puppy.

He winced at the memory of his brother taking him back to their native Yorkshire after he was beaten by a gang of thieves on his way back to his lodgings one night. He was still recovering when Georgia's marriage to Lord Edgar Jascombe was announced. What else could he do after that except bury his nose in his books and study for a degree when kicking up larks to forget that he loved her didn't work.

Now he was about to start a new life as the owner of neglected Holdfast Castle and estate in another county. But all the way here he had tried not to wonder when Lady Edgar Jascombe would stop mourning her late husband and realise Max wasn't an overgrown schoolboy any more. Then he saw her, so remote and pale in her widow's weeds yesterday, and was ashamed of himself. She still slipped him that note, though, so what did she want and where the devil was she?

He had a long, hard ride ahead of him and she should have better things to do than meet him when the sun was barely up and it was so damned cold his fingers and toes ached. Suddenly there she was, stepping out of the shadows as if she was part of them, and she looked so fragile and so very different from the merry, headlong girl he once knew.

'What is it, my lady?' he said when she was close enough for him to see dark shadows under her eyes as she pushed up her veil.

'My lady?' she echoed, as if she disliked the distance he was trying to put between them. 'I had to see you, Max,' she added.

'Why?'

She hesitated, as if wondering whether to say what she had come to say or go away again without doing it. 'Because *you* are a good man,' she said shakily.

Was he and why did she need him to be one? Horror swept over him as he suddenly saw the truth behind Georgia's splendid society marriage. She didn't look as if she hadn't slept or eaten for days because she was mourning her husband; she was guiltily relieved that Jascombe was dead.

'The cur you married wasn't a good one, was he?' he asked as gently as he could with so much fury and guilt and this old, frustrated love still raging inside him.

'No, he was a vile brute. I had to pretend I was happy in public or it would be worse for me later. When Millie was born I was afraid he would lash out at her because he hated being the father of a mere girl. Then there was a new one to be frightened for and he was even more furious she was born.'

She paused as if struggling to control emotions she had kept to herself too long. 'Oh, Max, I can't tell you how many times I have wished Edgar dead. What if I cursed him to die like that?'

'He would have died harder and a lot more slowly if wishing was all it took,' he told her grimly. He wanted death to have come slowly and painfully to the cur now he knew Jascombe was one.

No, calling him a cur was too good for him and a quick, clean death from a broken neck was too kind for Lord Edgar Jascombe. Georgia's mouth trembled as if she wanted to cry because Max believed in her and of course he did. He cursed the louse for putting shadows in her glorious eyes and he could see her hands were shaking.

It felt as if she would break if he pushed for facts, but why had she kept Jascombe's wickedness quiet for three years? She pushed a russet-gold curl off her face with an unsteady hand and his rage at a dead man nearly came out in a bellow of anguish because she had suffered and he hadn't known.

'I just wanted him gone,' she whispered.

'Did you try to kill him?'

'No, I didn't have the courage,' she said bleakly and met his eyes as if she was confessing to a terrible crime.

'You would have done if he went for your girls. I know you would fight for them with your last breath,' he said. He was so proud of her, but so frustrated she hadn't told him when the brute was alive. He cursed aloud because his rage felt so huge he couldn't keep it inside any longer. 'Not you, him,' he said when she flinched.

'I know,' she said, 'you were always on my side.'

'That's why you didn't tell me, isn't it?'

'Yes,' she said with a great sigh and walked into his arms.

He had often dreamt of her doing so, but never like this. He felt helpless and furious and such wrenching, frustrated pity for the violence and loneliness of her married life. She had finally let her guard down and he spared a little pity for himself because he knew he still loved her and it was even more hopeless than it was last time.

'A stern old god could have listened,' she said wildly.

'Someone would have noticed if he was struck by a thunderbolt from Olympus and it sounds as if he was just being his usual arrogant self when he forced his horse to jump a fence everyone else was avoiding.'

'The Duke did say the huntsmen shouted warnings, but Edgar said they were a pack of old women. His poor horse had to be shot, you know? I felt sorrier about that than Edgar's death, so I must be wicked.'

'He was the wicked one and you can dance on his grave if you like, but don't you dare feel guilty when he treated you so badly. *I* hope he roasts in hell for eternity.'

'He was the father of my children, though, Max, and I sat by his coffin the night before last and couldn't shed a tear.'

'Which proves you are already living better without him,' he said and wished it was true. She was so gaunt and pale, felt so fragile in his arms, he wondered if she would ever recover from three years of abuse by her own husband.

'Even after seeing him still as a waxwork I couldn't believe it was over, Max, but maybe I will now I have told you; I might stop feeling my life is a lie.'

'How long have you been keeping his nasty little secrets, then?'

'He hit me now and again from the outset, except when I was with child. He never came near when I was *enceinte*, but he certainly didn't hold back after Millie was born. Little Helen is only six weeks old, so I had to be churched after he died and at least he hasn't been near me like that for months now.'

She gave a great shiver and hid her face in his riding jacket and Max folded the front of his greatcoat around her and prayed she wasn't as broken as she seemed. He felt so guilty about staying away now, as if he had stood and watched the brute attack her and held his coat. He had been so busy protecting his own jealous, aching heart that he had never stopped to wonder if she was truly happy with her brilliant social catch.

'I'm so sorry, Georgia,' he told the top of her prickly dark bonnet.

He wanted to untie its grim ribbons, throw the dratted thing away and make sure she never had to wear mourning for Jascombe again, but how would she explain losing it? She didn't need whispers that she had met a lover the day after she buried her husband. He could almost hear Jascombe's mocking ghost say she would never want another man after him, but this wasn't about Max hating a dead man, it was about her.

'*You* have nothing to apologise for,' she whispered, refusing to look up. Maybe she was crying; she needed to after holding so much in for so long. 'I refused to see evil under Edgar's charm and he was the son of a duke, you see? Mama had always wanted me to marry well and the other debutantes were so jealous.'

Never mind a pack of giddy girls, Georgia's mother was keen to tell anyone who would listen that her genteel family fortunes had sunk so low she was forced to marry money. It said more about her than her husband, in his opinion, and Max had always liked Georgia's gentle father more than her pushy mother.

Right now he almost hated the silly woman for raising her only child to believe a fine society marriage and title were essential to her happiness. At eighteen Max had been the second son of a viscount without any hope of the tumbledown castle and estate that he was about to begin work on and *he* wasn't good enough for Mrs Welland, even if Georgia had loved him back and, sadly, she didn't.

'It wasn't your fault,' he said fiercely. 'Hurting you, expecting you to cover it up in public wasn't your wrong, it was his. He was the lowest of the low and never mind whose bed he was born in.'

'But I was such a *fool*, I should have married—'

'There's no point looking back at paths you didn't

take,' he interrupted since he didn't want to know who she wished she had married instead.

He could almost feel her fighting for the steely poise it must have taken to pretend she was happy in public and endure the rat's violence in private. He felt her lose the battle and felt helpless as he held her as she cried, as if all the fear and confusion pent up inside her had finally found a way out. He cursed the fates for not killing Jascombe before he could hurt a hair on her head and whispered whatever comfort he could think of.

'I shall never marry again,' she told him. She finally drew away and scrubbed her eyes dry with his handkerchief, then handed it back because her maid might find it and wonder whose it was. 'What do *you* live for, Max?'

'My family and a tumbledown castle in Northumberland that nobody else wants.'

'You always did pick up waifs and strays,' she said with such a gallant attempt at a smile he almost cried, too. 'Thank you for meeting me, Max. It was kind of you to listen to my woes and let me cry all over you like a weeping willow.'

'I will always listen if you need me to, Georgia. I shall be at Holdfast Castle, trying to make order out of the chaos its last owner created if you need to talk about it again.'

'When your mother wrote to me she said you were deciding whether to take it on. She doesn't sound very happy about the idea,' she said as if she needed to make small talk.

Max shoved his hands in his greatcoat pockets to hide his clenched fists because she was setting him at a distance again. 'She thinks my paternal grand-mother's obsession with her ancestral home has al-ready cost her much too dear,' he said. 'But never mind that sad old story, promise you will come and see me there if you need to talk about him again, Georgia?' he insisted with three years of wilful ig-norance prodding at his conscience.

'I will—now goodbye and God speed. Thank you for proving me right,' she said and walked back into the shadowy wood as if he had imagined her.

Right about what? Ah, yes, Max the good man— what a lie he was.

Chapter One

Summer 1815

'It's only going to be for six weeks, Georgia,' Miss Leonora Haverstock, her children's governess, said, but it felt like for ever.

'How does my father-in-law think taking my girls back to Mynham will help me get better from the influenza, Leonora? Missing them and worrying about them living under their grandparents' roof for the next month and a half will make me feel worse.'

'He is right, though. You are still pale and you have lost weight and as you were feverish for nearly a fortnight even I was worried about you,' Leonora replied cheerfully. But Georgia suspected she was dreading six weeks at stiff and stately Mynham with two lively young pupils to keep out of the Duke and Duchess of Ness's way.

Edgar had named his father as his children's guardian in his will so Georgia had to give in when the Duke refused to be talked out of this plan for her to recover in peace, as if it would be anything of the kind. Edgar's last cruelty against her stung afresh as she had no choice but to go along with the Duke's ridiculous idea for her to convalesce alone.

'I was feeling so much better when the Duke called on his way back from Brussels with news of the Allied victory at Waterloo, but then I started to cough and couldn't stop. He seems to think I will be a permanent invalid if he doesn't interfere, but I'm as strong as an ox.'

'Maybe you are, but you don't look it right now. You probably do need to breathe clean air and get plenty of rest.'

'Perhaps,' Georgia conceded with a glance out of the window at the usual haze over the city, which gave it a yellowish tint even on a fine day, 'but not without my girls. I will just worry about them under the Duke's roof without me.'

'I don't suppose he knows how a true mother feels about her children, Georgia, since the Duchess doesn't strike me as the maternal type, although everyone says she doted on your late husband so maybe I am misjudging her.'

'No, she could hardly ignore her elder son and spoil the younger one if she cared about them, but I suppose you're right and the Duke truly doesn't realise I love my children dearly,' Georgia said with a sigh. 'He is always accusing me of spoiling them, but you know how careful I am not to do so. I'm so afraid he will decide I am an unfit mother and not give them back to me.'

'Oh, for goodness sake, Georgia, stop imagining the worst and concentrate on getting better so you can convince him you must have us all back here soon. In the meantime Nanny and I will care for them as if they are our own and the weeks will fly by. It makes sense for you to leave the city until it is cooler and the air is cleaner.'

'I suppose I might as well,' Georgia said listlessly. 'I know you will do your best to stop them being glowered at by their grandfather or petted by their grandmother, but they are a duke and duchess, don't forget.'

'And I am the daughter of a bishop. Even His Grace seems in awe of my saintly papa's spiritual authority as opposed to his temporal kind,' Leonora said with a fond smile and Georgia wondered all over again why her friend had left the Bishop's Palace to become even a very superior governess.

When she had interviewed her Leonora said she didn't want to marry and, as she didn't want to devote her life to good works either, she had given teaching a try and found out that she enjoyed it. Georgia suspected there was a lot more to Leonora's story, but didn't want to pry. She was so lucky Leonora was very good at her job and had become a friend as well.

'You have already taught my girls more than they

wanted to know so my father-in-law should approve of you,' she told her.

'Having a bishop in the family helps and I dare say it's the main reason you employed me in the first place,' Leonora replied with a rueful smile.

'It did help convince the Duke that Millie and Helen were in safe hands, but the main reason I chose you was because I like you.'

'Thank you, I like you, too—especially when you are not being such a tragedienne as you are today and imagining the worst.'

'Stop trying to cheer me up when I don't want to be cheered, Leonora. Today I want to throw things and lose my temper and have the hysterics like my mother-in-law does when her life doesn't run exactly as she expects it to.'

'You are not helping me look forward to a month and a half at Mynham.'

'I know, but if I hadn't been so foolish as to get the influenza at a ridiculous time of year we would all be in Weymouth by now. Staying there with you and my girls would do me far more good than wandering about the country missing them ever will. I know it's not a fashionable watering place nowadays, but the girls love the sea and sand.

'Oh, ignore me. I know it's no good talking about it because the Duke won't hear of that idea and I can't go there on my own.' Even thinking about it started another coughing fit. 'Confounded cough!' she spluttered as Leonora passed her a glass of the lemonade

Cook had made so often that Georgia wondered the markets hadn't run out of lemons yet.

'Trust me to look after them and concentrate on getting better, Georgia,' Leonora said when she finally managed to stop and sat back, feeling dispirited and exhausted.

'I do trust you, but the Duke has no idea how little girls think or behave. His only concern is they don't cause him any trouble or besmirch the precious Jascombe name in any way.'

'How could a few childish misdeeds do that?'

'I don't know,' Georgia said miserably, but after spending most of her marriage under their roof she knew the Jascombes' ideas of proper behaviour were skewed.

'The Duke is always watching for proof they will follow in their father's footsteps one day. He knows Edgar had a twisted soul, although he would not dream of admitting it out loud. He thinks it's his duty to make sure the taint isn't passed on to Edgar's daughters.'

Six months after she employed her she had told Leonora why she was so intent on not spoiling her girls so she would understand why Georgia was stricter with them than she wanted to be. At least Leonora knew why she didn't want her girls to suffer a repeat of their father's peculiar upbringing under the Duke's roof. That was why Georgia lived in London, close enough to Mynham for the Duke to believe he was keeping an eye on them, far enough away to stop him interfering in their day-to-day lives.

Sometimes it was too close, though, and she had always dreaded the Duke would decide she might as well live at Mynham instead so he could keep a keener eye on her and her daughters. The idea of ever having to do so again made her shudder even when she wasn't ill and set off yet another coughing fit now.

'Then he worries too much and so do you,' Leonora said bracingly. 'Your girls have such good natures under the mischief. I am sure they are nothing like their father and more like you.'

'Thank you, but it's the mischief that concerns me. The Duke thinks little girls should sew samplers and learn insipid accomplishments and never speak unless they are spoken to, but it's the Duchess I am really worried about. She will try to spoil them until they think nobody else's pleasures matter but theirs, like their father. Promise to stop her treating them like lapdogs because they are Edgar's children and never mind if he hated fathering girls.'

'I will try, but don't you think they would be bored in half a day if Her Grace tried it?'

'True,' Georgia said ruefully. 'Thank you for being so patient with me, Leonora. I do know how annoying I am being and none of this is your fault.'

'You have been ill so I shall graciously forgive you this once, but I can hear the Duke's men and horses are getting restless so we really must go now.'

Georgia insisted on seeing them off and never mind her slightly wobbly legs and any other symptoms her stupid illness had left behind. Despite the fears that refused to die after Leonora's reassurances, Georgia kissed her girls and hugged them and told them they would enjoy themselves at Mynham. Then she stood in the street, frantically smiling and waving until the Duke's second-best travelling carriage had turned out of the quiet street where they lived and was lost to sight.

That was when she let her shoulders droop and went back to her silent and empty-feeling town house and six weeks felt like six years. As soon as she heard the clock ticking in the silence she knew she couldn't stay here alone and rang for her maid.

'It's too late to find decent lodgings in Brighton and I can't endure Weymouth without my girls, so we might as well go to Yorkshire and stay with my parents for a week or so, Huggins.'

'By easy stages, my lady,' her maid said with a sharp look at Georgia's pale face and teary eyes.

'Oh, yes, we wouldn't want to risk me having a relapse, would we?'

'No, my lady, we would not,' Huggins said with surprising firmness.

Her maid must be worried to have let even a hint of feeling show. Huggins had done such a good job of keeping those to herself during Georgia's marriage that perhaps the Duke was right and she really did look ill.

'If you can be ready for us to depart by tomorrow morning, we might as well begin our leisurely journey home to Riverdale as soon as we can so I can cosset myself like an invalid,' she said listlessly.

'Yes, my lady,' Huggins said in her usual impassive way.

Georgia knew she was being silently rebuked for making light of her illness and what would be their first visit to her old home in four years. Going back downstairs while Huggins got on with packing in peace, Georgia stared moodily out of the drawing room windows and wondered how it would feel to be in her old home and not see Max every day. She had done so most days when they were growing up.

His brother's land ran alongside her father's more modest acres and the two of them had run wild over both estates as children and had all sorts of adventures behind their parents' backs. Max would be busy at Holdfast Castle even further north as he tried to make good the damage its previous owner had done to the poor old place.

The idea of staying in her old home when he wasn't nearby felt so wrong that she wasn't sure she even wanted to be there without him, but there was nowhere else she wanted to be so she might as well go there. Max would have listened to her worries and made her feel better, but he wasn't there any more. She couldn't tell her parents about them, either, since she hadn't confided in them at the time.

Yet she couldn't stay here listening to the silence

either, so she sighed mournfully and decided she must have faith in Leonora and just make sure she was well enough to take charge of her daughters again at the end of summer.

It had felt so odd to be home, yet not feel at home there, Georgia decided as her neat carriage took the detour she had impulsively ordered the coachman to make when she saw a sign pointing to the nearest town to Holdfast. Riverdale Manor had felt familiar and so strange without Max this last week and she had been glad to leave it for a visit to Aunt Isobel, her father's sister, who lived in Edinburgh.

Her parents were much as they had always been— her mother still thought she had married beneath her and her father endured being her wealthy, but not very convenient, husband with his usual patience and far too much humility.

Max's brother Zachary, Viscount Elderwood, and his unconventional wife were in Cumberland with her maternal grandparents so Flaxonby itself was shut up and looking a bit forlorn.

At Flaxonby Dower House Max's mother, the Dowager Viscountess Elderwood, was preoccupied with her grief-stricken younger daughter Becky and Becky's five-month-old baby girl. Becky's beloved Captain Jack Sothern had been killed at the terrible battle near Waterloo and she was inconsolable.

Georgia felt guilty on two counts about her brief visit to the Dower House. First, because she had been secretly delighted when her own mother had gone home after Edgar had died so Georgia could stop pretending to her nearest and dearest; second, because she was glad Becky was too devastated by that tragedy to see anyone.

The two of them had never got on and had less in common than ever now, yet if she had stayed at Riverdale much longer they would have been lumped together as bereft young widows. She might have been expected to know how to comfort Becky in her first appalling grief, but Becky was mourning a husband she adored. Pretending she understood would make Georgia a hypocrite.

Staying at Riverdale had made her realise how much she had changed since she left it as a naive young woman intent on making the fine marriage her mother had always dreamt of for her. She knew how mistaken her mother was in thinking a title and ancient bloodlines made for a good marriage now and she felt impatient with the comparisons Mrs Welland kept on making between her own genteel family and her husband's supposedly humble one.

Marriage to an aristocrat had taught her rank was just names, power and wealth, so her mother's objections wouldn't stop Georgia from visiting her darling Aunt Isobel now she was in the north. Aunt Isobel's late husband had been a merchant who did business with Georgia's grandfather, so of course Mama thought the connection was undesirable, but

Georgia had always loved her stays with Aunt Isobel as a child.

Now her aunt was a widow and a devoted grandmother. She had always welcomed Georgia into her fine home to enjoy the delights of the Scottish capital for a week or two and forget the stuffy southerners her brother had married into. Georgia had always secretly liked Papa's family much better than her mother's staid and self-important relatives.

Papa was a good and gentle husband and her mother had been lucky to have stumbled on one of those more or less by accident when she was on the lookout for a wealthy catch. Would that her daughter had been so fortunate when she blundered into marriage for all the wrong reasons as well.

Georgia stared out of the carriage window at a heavily wooded landscape that told her they were not on the Holdfast Estate yet since so many mature trees had been felled by the previous owner it was easy to tell when you were on Holdfast land. So she could go back to thinking how uncomfortable it had felt at Riverdale with her parents as divided by stupid differences in birth and rank as ever.

She had no right to upset the status quo the two of them had established when she had no idea how a real marriage should run. Maybe that was why it was such a relief to get away from Riverdale and all that was the same and should be different. It was probably why she was so restless there, not because Max no longer lived next door as he had when they were children. She was on her way to see him, but he was her best friend when they were young so it would be rude *not* to call when she was passing.

All of a sudden Max's grim northern stronghold was looming on the horizon and she must have been wool-gathering not to notice the trees thin out, then disappear except for a few ragged stands of birch and alder the previous owner must have been unable to sell. There were signs of Max's care for his beloved acres in sapling woods planted on less productive acres, but it would be decades before they provided shelter and centuries before they were mature and he had only been here five years.

Holdfast was visible long before it would have been before all saleable trees were felled and even the most fanciful debutante would not see it as a fairy tale palace now. Perhaps that was why Max hadn't been snapped up by an eager young lady with Holdfast Castle looking so dour and forbidding they didn't want to live there. Max obviously loved it and must have become immune to the chill winds that would whistle around it for much of the year.

She shivered at the thought of living here when winter came, so she must have gone soft living in the south. London seemed very far away today and she had been drawn to her native north since she got here, but nowhere felt like a home without her girls.

She knew Millie and Helen were safe and cared for with Leonora and their nanny, but as Holdfast loomed ever closer Georgia knew she was a bad mother because she wanted her daughters to be missing her nearly as much as she did them. She shifted against the comfortable squabs and stared at the stronghold of Max's ancestors to try to forget how selfish she was.

Max had put a great deal of work into the stony old place since she last called here on her way to Aunt Isobel's four years ago. How happy they had been to get out of the carriage for a while when Helen was eighteen months old and even Millie was only three going on four. Back then the journey north had felt endless even with Nanny's help and Georgia had resolved not to do it again until they were bigger and easier to keep amused.

When they had got here they had toddled gamely around a real castle with delighted squeals and chuckles for the giant play house Mama had brought them to so there was no chance to talk to her old friend properly, which had suited her perfectly. She should have come back sooner, though. If she had done so, maybe she would not have been in London to contract a stupid illness this spring and her daughters would have loved to visit a real castle even more than they did when they were little.

To stop missing them so bitterly, she watched the sun shine on renewed roofs and repaired windows. A pleasure garden was being rescued from the undergrowth that had still engulfed the sheltered side of the castle the last time she was here. She wondered if Max would love this place less and leave it more often if he wasn't a grandson of the last of the De-Mayne line and a splendid heiress when she married Max's grandfather, the spendthrift Lord Elderwood who had gambled his wife's grand heritage away along with most of his own.

She missed her oldest friend and had only just realised she resented this place for keeping him hundreds of miles away from her. There she was again, being selfish, when she should be glad he had found such a strong purpose in life. She had her girls to give her life meaning, but without them it felt hollow. She shook her head, furious with herself for the self-pity behind that depressing thought.

Maybe she had taken this diversion with a sneaky hope she could unburden herself to him again, but she had burdened him with too many problems in the past and he was a busy man. She practised her best social smile in her reflection in the carriage window and decided twenty minutes would be quite long enough to call on an unrelated gentleman. Nobody could accuse her of ignoring an old friend while she was passing now and she could get to the part of this enforced holiday she was actually looking forward to as soon as that time was up.

Max hammered the final nail into the last new oak floorboard and sat back on his heels to survey his handiwork. As soon as they were stained to match the originals nobody would know the rain had got in through a broken window and spoiled some of them. His little sister's new home was a step closer to being ready. Perhaps he could afford to hire a carpenter now the estate was beginning to pay its way, but when he had first come here he had to learn skills a gentleman wasn't supposed to and he enjoyed this one. The physical effort of his life here had been the perfect fit for him when he agreed to take it on five years ago.

He shrugged off the memory of Georgia weeping in his arms the day after Jascombe's funeral. He had spent too many days working like a demon to get her and her wretched marriage out of his head and heart back then and he was done with wanting what he couldn't have. He was glad his younger sister Becky had asked to share his home so she and her baby daughter could have a new start somewhere without any deep connection to her darling Jack.

It would be a new beginning for him as well. Not that he wanted to leave Holdfast, but he had to stop yearning for impossible things. He loved this place as he never thought he would when he accepted it from his brother and sister-in-law, mainly because it seemed to need him as much as he needed something worthwhile to do.

Working hard on it had stopped him having sleepless nights or dreaming that Georgia needed him again and he couldn't get to her in his nightmares. Five years on he belonged in this sometimes harsh, always beautiful land as he never had in his brother's grand neo-classical mansion. Max had no vocation for the church and had never wanted to join the army or navy and see the world while fighting his fellow man, but Holdfast had been so forlorn it called out to him. Yes, it was time to put the past behind him.

He needed to find a wife to run it and share his life, someone in tune with his hopes and dreams who wanted to hear their children chase up and down the corridors and play hide and seek in Holdfast's quirky corners. Becky's little girl should not play alone when she was big enough to and it was time he came fully alive along with his castle. It was good enough now to ask a hardy lady to share his life and ancient home. He just needed to find one who was happy to raise their children in less splendour than his DeMayne ancestors had kept in Holdfast's glory days.

Chapter Two

'Max. Max! Where are you hiding yourself? A boy in the courtyard said I was to follow the sound of hammering and I'd find you, but it's stopped and it can't have been you.'

'Georgia! What are you doing here?' He dropped his hammer as if it was red hot and jumped up to greet her with such joy in his heart he had best not examine it too deeply.

'It *was* you knocking in nails like a peasant just now then. Whatever have they done to you, my dear?' she said and smiled like a vision from his wildest dreams.

She wasn't strictly beautiful, he supposed numbly, but that didn't matter. She had redefined beauty for him long ago and nobody else had her unique combination of russet-gold curls and eyes of a clear lavender-blue set in a heart-shaped face.

Best stop there, Chilton.

He didn't want to linger over a temptingly full

top lip or the lithe feminine figure shown off by her very fashionable gown. He had tried so hard to think of her as just a friend for so long now that he could just about manage it when she didn't surprise him.

'But nowadays I knock them in like an artisan,' he replied as lightly as he could manage, 'and that's a step up from a peasant, don't you think?'

'Oh, no, Max, thinking is *so* wearisome and it would give me lines.'

'You might fool the rest of the *ton* you don't have two thoughts to rub together in your lovely head, but there's no point in trying to convince me as well. I grew up with you so I know what a devious little devil you are.'

'And you were such a horrid brat you tried to leave me behind for all your best adventures.'

Max thought they were almost too good at this game of *Let's pretend we have nothing serious to say to one another.*

'Only because you used to squeak like a baby bird and give us away,' he obliged her anyway.

'I was excited,' she said with a dignified look that should have made him ashamed of his boyhood self, but he was too busy worrying about his grown-up one to bother.

She had never felt the same yearning for him as he had for her from the first moment he had seen her with her wild curls tamed and put up like a proper society lady and her skirts so demure she looked nothing like her usual harum-scarum self. She was being led into dinner by the most important young gentleman in the area at the time.

That was the day he learned how to be jealous of his own brother, since Zach was Viscount Elderwood by then and the young nobleman chosen to take the newly fledged daughter of the house in to dinner. Luckily Zach was unmoved by Georgia's sudden transformation into a young lady so it didn't last long. Max wondered about his brother's eyesight, but had been delighted when Zach disappointed Mrs Welland's finest ambition for her daughter in the local area. He reminded himself that was a very long time ago now.

Georgia was looking around the empty, but newly sound room as if she had never seen the like before and she probably hadn't. Riverdale Manor was immaculately maintained and he was sure not an inch of Mynham dared be shabby with Ness keeping a close eye on it.

'Are you planning to repair this entire castle on your own, Max?' she asked lightly. She turned to stare out of the window at his parkland as if she was only here to inspect his progress and he knew that bit wasn't very impressive.

'It would take half a dozen lifetimes if I was fool enough to try, but I like doing some of it myself when I have the time.'

'I doubt you have much to spare.' She turned to look at him again with the real smile he recalled from childhood lighting her face to true beauty. He reminded himself not to fall in love with her all over again. 'I have never thanked you for being a good friend when I needed one, Max. I always did trust you with my darkest secrets, didn't I?'

'You know they are all safe with me.'

'Thank you.'

She went back to watching his not very fascinating parkland and she was still a little too good at hiding her feelings behind a serene expression nowadays. Not that he wanted her to tell him about any more of them when last time had hurt so much. In that godforsaken copse at Mynham five years ago he had hated Jascombe so fiercely he didn't feel cold all the way back here for the fire and futility of it all burning inside him. The brute had treated her so badly it killed any hope he had Georgia might come to love him back one day.

Not that it mattered now because Max was done with loving her. He hadn't dreamt of her lovely eyes hazy with love and desire for him for months now. Of course, he was eager to find his kind and sensible Mrs Chilton instead of indulging in old fantasies of her as deep in love with him as he had been with her. He would get on with his new life as soon as Becky was settled and her grief less raw and he had forgotten Lady Edgar Jascombe again. He was so good at it now it shouldn't take nearly as long as it did last time.

'Come and see what a fine job my gardener and stable boys have made of the old pleasance, Georgia.' He had to get her out of a too intimate-feeling room, even if it didn't have a bed in it yet. 'That way the tabbies can't shake their heads at us being alone in here if they find out you have been visiting without a chaperon.'

'They would have to know about it first and your men don't look as if they indulge in idle gossip,' she said lightly, but led the way downstairs anyway. 'You do good work, Max,' she said as she peeped into the rooms he had already repaired for his sister in this Tudor dwelling house that had been built inside the old walls for some relative too important to consign to a draughty tower and forget about. 'This will be a fine place for your sister and niece to make their home when it's finished.'

'I hope so. She needs to be able to come and go as she pleases so I want to get the Little House repaired as soon as possible.'

'Yes, poor Becky, she must be devastated by her loss,' Georgia said with a sad shake of her head at the true grief of a loving wife for a loving husband.

He was glad when they were outside again and he shrugged his battered old coat back on despite the sunshine and the light breeze. He knew what was due to a lady and that wasn't a working man in shirtsleeves, dusty and maybe a little sweaty from his labours. For a while they walked in silence as he thought of love and grief and didn't want to talk about her lack of either for *her* late husband.

'Goodness, this entire area was covered in brambles and ivy and old man's beard last time I was here,' she said as he opened the garden door and the scent of the roses in bloom was sweet on the summer air.

'That was four years ago,' he said.

He recalled the exact time and day she had come and how preoccupied she was with her family, but he didn't want her to know he remembered every second of her hasty visit. He wondered why she had bothered to come that day, but it was probably to let him know she *was* preoccupied with her children so he had no need to worry about her any more. He wasn't sure if that had been a kindness or more unconscious cruelty when he had been struggling so hard to forget her again, but it hardly mattered when they were little more than polite strangers now.

'True and, although you never come to London, my parents do, so I don't need to come north very often in order to see them.'

'I know,' he said shortly. They crossed the walled gardens and went through the gate to the old pleasance, where long-dead DeMayne ladies had once escaped the stern reality of living in a stronghold to stroll and play games and dream a little.

He loved the view of the hills beyond and liked to think some of the ancient herbs and wildflowers were left over from the days when Holdfast was young and home to fighting DeMaynes and their dependents. He could picture the old place, busy and noisy with fighting men training and myriads of servants to look after a garrison and the old lords' chosen retainers and family. This must have been a quiet sanctuary from all that busyness once upon a time and he liked to fancy one or two of those ladies still kept a silent watch over it.

Now he was trying to distract himself from Georgia's presence by wondering about this place in its heyday and it was never going to work with her faint perfume teasing his senses. Her frothy summer gown clung to far too many of her feminine curves for his comfort as that playful breeze outlined her figure and she didn't seem to realise it. Because of Jascombe's cruelty she was oddly innocent about her own charms and unease ran under his reluctant admiration of them as that ignorance felt dangerous for her.

'Edgar secretly hated all the history and tradition at Mynham, you know? I'm glad you treasure the past as well as the present,' she said and looked as if she wished she hadn't reminded herself she was once married to the rat.

'I'm sorry you can't forget him, Georgia' Max said impulsively.

'Don't you dare be sorry for me,' she snapped back fiercely and that was more like the Georgia he once knew.

'That's not what I said and I *am* sorry that you feel you can't trust another man. There are plenty of good ones in the world and very few of us enjoy inflicting pain.' She looked sceptical. 'Refuse to live freely and joyfully and he wins, Georgia,' he cautioned.

'He can't; he's dead and I wouldn't trust myself to

know a good man from a bad one even if I wanted another husband and I don't,' she said, gazing at that view to avoid looking at him.

The fool he once was flinched at her denial of interest in any man, least of all him. 'You were very young and Jascombe acted his part well,' he said.

'I thought all men were like you so I had nothing to fear from him, but I was so wrong. I could kick myself for being so easily taken in.'

'Don't make your marriage to a noble rat be my fault, Georgia!'

'I'm sorry; I didn't mean to hurt your feelings.'

'No, you never do.'

There was a tense pause and she looked as if she was getting ready to march away in a huff. He almost wished she would.

'I don't mean it was your fault I married him, idiot,' she argued brusquely, 'just that you have such a good heart, despite being a rough-and-tumble boy and sometimes treating me as a mere girl when we were young. You taught me to expect that all men would be like you, that's all; I didn't look past Edgar's surface charm and realise he was your opposite in every way that counted.'

Max wanted to hit something, although he knew it wouldn't solve anything, or help her say whatever she really came to say, so he held his fury at the idea her marriage was his fault in any way inside with a mighty effort. 'And now you know how to spot a fake you will be able to choose better next time,' he said as casually as he could manage.

'I shall never marry again,' she insisted with a shudder.

Yet he could see she wasn't happy and he still loved her enough to want her to be so. 'Never is a long time,' he said carefully, 'and are you ever going to tell me why you really came out of your way to see me?'

'Because I wanted to see you again, of course, and it was time I inspected your progress here. It is very impressive.'

He let his impatience show. He needed to know why she was looking so drawn and thin again. 'Thank you,' he said blandly, refusing to fill the silence with polite chatter.

'Oh, very well,' she said at last with a gusty sigh. 'I contracted the influenza at the beginning of June. The Duke called on me on his way home from Brussels with news of the battle, since rumours were flying around that the Allies had been defeated and he knew I would be worried for my daughters' safety. He caught me in the middle of a coughing fit and decided I was more ill than I would admit so he has carried my girls back to Mynham with him for weeks and weeks while I recover to his satisfaction.'

'It is hot and airless in London at this time of year—I wonder any of you can breathe even when you are in rude health,' he said despite the anxiety pricking at him because she had been so ill even Ness had noticed.

'You don't understand,' she said sulkily.

He didn't want to. He wanted her to storm off in a temper and never come back, but she was his old friend and must have a reason for coming out of her way to see him. He had to get her to tell him what was troubling her and hope it wasn't too dreadful. 'Explain it to me better, then,' he said.

'I can't sleep for worrying about my girls living at Mynham without me,' she admitted at last.

'They are only visiting their grandparents,' he argued, 'and Ness is right for once. You do need to recover properly and it makes sense for them to stay there until you are truly well again.'

She shook her head and looked as if she wished she hadn't bothered to come if that was all he had to say. 'You don't understand,' she accused him again, but a lot more crossly this time. At least that was better than the wistful look in her eyes when she talked of her daughters being kept at Mynham by their top-lofty grandfather.

'No, I don't,' he said. 'There must be more keeping you awake than worry about their routine being disrupted. Are you tempted to let some man into your life although you don't think you want to, Georgia? Is that why you really came to see me after so long?'

He couldn't think why else she had broken four years of near silence and this wasn't jealousy ripping through him like a rusty saw. He wouldn't let it be and she didn't want to marry him today any more than she had done eight years ago.

If only he had found the courage, or the words, to tell her there was nothing he wanted more back then, they might both be very different people today, but that was just a pipe dream. He still had to find his perfect Mrs Chilton and she would have to be nothing like Lady Edgar Jascombe, society widow and leader of fashion, if she was going to be happy here year in and year out.

Georgia shuddered at the idea of another man with the right to do whatever he wanted to her whenever he wanted to. Did Max really think she had come here to ask for his advice on such an impossible subject? How could he when he knew the truth about her marriage to Edgar? It felt as if he was wishing her away, as if they were almost strangers, and that hurt.

'Of course not,' she said, 'and four years isn't so very long.'

'True,' he said indifferently.

How stupid to want him to have missed her when she was the one who had stayed away. 'The finest wife is less than the worst husband in the eyes of the law, so why would I walk into that trap twice?' she said and breathed in deeply and slowly to calm her jumping nerves.

His silence and averted gaze said he was fighting with his own strong feelings and he *was* a man so she supposed she had insulted him along with the rest. She held her breath, fearing their long friendship had finally been broken and it would be her fault.

'Not all marriages are bleak as yours was, Georgia,' he argued and she let out a quiet sigh of relief because at least he still cared enough to argue. 'Ask my sister-in-law if she feels less because she is married to Zach. Seeing them together at the last ball you all attended should have shown you that you're wrong if you did think it.'

Zachary's spirited wife clearly adored her husband, but she was never likely to submit to husbandly authority and Zachary would not ask her to.

'I do know that happy marriages exist,' she conceded, 'and your brother and sister-in-law clearly have one so there's no need to frown at me as if I'm being irrational. Edgar showed me that wicked men can pretend to be good and kind, though, so it's not sensible of me to risk myself and my daughters by trusting one again, so kindly stop reasoning with me in that infuriating way, Maxwell Chilton.'

'Max,' he argued with an old boyish impatience that almost made her cry for some strange reason. Her illness must have been more debilitating than she thought for her to still be so tearful weeks afterwards.

'Your mother only called you Maxwell when she was taking you to task for our mischief when we were children, so I don't wonder you dislike it,' she said with a wry smile.

'It was usually your mischief as well.'

'True,' she said and felt better about being born female.

Yet Max was so very grown up and male now she couldn't lose herself in the safe past for very long. He had grown into such a strong man while her back was turned. How silly of her not to have waited for him to grow up when they were both eighteen instead of blithely marrying Edgar as if he was about to make all her dreams come true. She recalled how she and Max were back then and nearly laughed at the very idea he could have loved her if only they had tried hard enough.

Now he managed to look very dashing even in workman's boots, frayed shirt and old leathers topped with a coat most gentlemen's grooms would refuse to wear. Edgar had always dressed fashionably even when he was in the country, but somehow Max's disreputable old clothes gave him a presence Edgar's finery never managed to lend him. There was no need for a fine London tailor to pad *his* shoulders out when Max was so fit and muscular that the seams of the battered old coat he was wearing had snapped once or twice already and been mended so he could wear it when he was working.

Someone must patch it for the rough labour most gentlemen would never soil their hands with. She pictured some besotted seamstress bending over Max's mending, wishing he would wear her next to his skin instead of his overworked shirts and disreputable coat. Did he have a mistress? She thought he must do and couldn't understand why the very idea of one had set her teeth on edge.

She flinched away from being needed like that ever again, yet here she was wondering how Max's woman felt when all his sensual attention was centred on her. Georgia knew he would never humiliate or hurt a woman to make himself feel stronger and better and Max's bedazzled mistress probably longed for his quiet knock on her door to say never mind sleeping tonight.

A wondering shiver slid down her spine as she wished she knew how it felt to be needed by a good and strong man, but it turned icy at the thought of ever doing *that* again with any man. What had they been talking about before she let her thoughts stray into such an impossible place? Ah, yes, their childhood misdeeds and the punishments he took for them.

'I feel bad about our mischief now I'm a mother myself,' she said. 'Your poor mama had to put up with it while she was doing her best to bring you and Becky up alone after your father died so young. Even your elder sister Joan wasn't very old at the time and Zachary was a schoolboy and we caused them so much trouble.'

'You should feel guilty, considering your father would never punish you even if he caught us red-handed,' Max said. 'He would just shake his head and say he was disappointed in you, but if you had been born a boy you would have had to go without your supper nearly as often as I did.'

'True again,' she replied with a reminiscent smile.

The contrast between then and now felt so sharp it seemed to cut into her like knives. 'Ah, Max, sometimes I feel so lost,' she said impulsively, 'as if I'm living inside a picture and nothing in my life is quite real.'

Oh, confound it! Why had she let her tongue run away with her? She had shown him the absolute loneliness that sometimes bit into her even in a crowded room and he was already trying to put some distance between them. For a long moment he stared down at her as if he wanted to say something passionate and significant, but then he looked away again. When he looked back there was only compassion in his dark eyes and he led her to a finely made bench she suspected was his handiwork.

They sat and gazed at the lovely view from the top of what she guessed was once a flowery mead in the high medieval style. Of course she *had* been ill and the influenza must have affected her nerves more than she had thought, because the side closest to him was tingling as if she was being seared by a primal force. They had sat like this so many times when they were young it seemed ridiculous not to be at ease with him now.

She shifted a little further away from him and stared at the fine view in the hope it could soothe her stupid nerves. And that was all it could be, wasn't it? Just her upset nerves after all that worrying and sleepless nights. What else could it be?

'Nobody is more real than you are, Georgia,' he

argued softly at last and she decided she felt better now. It must have been a goose walking over her grave, one of those inexplicable changes of mood everyone suffered from time to time. 'Jascombe undermined you because he was a nonentity, but he's dead now and you're alive. It's time you saw yourself as you really are before he ruins your life from beyond the grave,' he added. She was so glad he hadn't noticed the blush she could feel cooling on her cheeks and had no idea she had trouble taking in his meaning before she pulled herself together.

'You really think he was a nonentity?' she said incredulously when it did hit her. Edgar had loomed so large in her life she had never been able to see him in such a cool, clear light before, but Max was right: he *did* look insignificant from here.

'Well, he did nothing with his life to prove he wasn't, did he? Even his own father disliked him and, while his mother may have mistakenly adored him, Lord Edgar Jascombe was born unimportant and he died the same way.'

'I suppose you're right.' She felt as if her life had just fallen into a new pattern, but she wasn't quite sure what it was yet.

'I still curse him to hell for trying to break you so he could feel better about himself, but at least he didn't succeed.'

'Didn't he? Sometimes I feel as if he did,' she admitted wearily.

Chapter Three

'You're the strongest woman I know, Georgia,' Max insisted because he couldn't hold her close and comfort her without wanting her and that was impossible for both of them.

'No, I'm weak,' she argued and now he was worried she would never recover from years of Jascombe chipping away her confidence.

'Do you think any woman would have survived a marriage like that unscathed?'

'He so nearly broke me.'

'But he didn't, did he? You acted so well nobody suspected what a beast he was in private. He must have hated the fact you were stronger inside than he was and he couldn't crush your spirit.'

'Maybe you're right,' she said as if coming to terms with something revolutionary.

'It has been known,' he said wryly, 'but that's enough about him. Are you going to tell me why you came here when there must be more exciting places for a fashionable lady to visit while she is on tour?'

'I had almost forgotten what you look like.'

'And we both know you don't want me visiting you,' he said flatly. 'I don't fit your world and I know too much about you.'

'I don't mean to be difficult, Max,' she said and he almost laughed because she was born difficult and he wouldn't have her any other way, despite the heartache she had caused him over the years.

'You never did, but why did you really come out of your way to see me, Georgia?'

'You are such a nag nowadays,' she said almost sulkily, but then her worries about Ness keeping her daughters came tumbling out and he was so astonished he wasn't insulted.

'So you have been making yourself miserable because Ness took your girls off your hands so that you could recuperate in peace?' he said incredulously.

'Don't make me sound so foolish, Max. Edgar made Ness their guardian so he can decide where they live and with whom.'

'They are females who have no place in the ducal succession. Why would he keep them close when they have a perfectly good mother to save him the bother?'

'Because they are Edgar's children and the Duchess will cling to them like a leech. She thought Edgar could do no wrong, so she won't care if they are girls; they are his children and she blindly adored him.'

'The Duke didn't adore him. My guess is he knew what a crooked dolt he had spawned. Ness is a bumbling idiot in many ways, but he has enough sense not to want that unsavoury bit of family history to be repeated.'

'Then why did he take my girls away and tell me that they can't come back until he says so?'

'*Because* he's a bumbling idiot, of course, and I expect he wants to make sure you are well enough to take them off his hands for good by the autumn. The last thing he will want then is a pair of lively young girls underfoot when his new grandchild is born.'

'Lord Chert's Marchioness is with child, then?' she asked incredulously, and Max nodded. 'Why didn't the Duke tell me and how do you know?'

'My godmother is Lady Chert's aunt and writes about all sorts of things to me that she probably should not because she knows I never go anywhere important to tattle about them.'

'Not that you would even if you didn't live in the middle of nowhere.'

'No, I'm too safe for my own good,' he said sourly, but Georgia wasn't listening.

'If his son and heir has finally got on and done his duty to the Duke's precious succession, maybe he really does only want me to be fit and well before the child is born.'

'Of course he does—Ness doesn't want your girls, Georgia. All he cares about is passing on his titles and possessions to the next heir until the end of time.'

'What about the Duchess?'

'What about her?' Max said cynically.

Given the damage the woman had done by spoiling her second son so much he grew up devious and selfish, he refused to pity a duchess with nothing to do but pretend she was important and worship the memory of her repellent son.

'Now Lady Chert is with child, I suppose the Duchess's whims and fancies will matter less than ever to her husband,' Georgia mused.

'She served her purpose and gave the Duke an heir and a spare, but he doesn't matter much to her either, so don't waste your pity. The Duchess of Ness is the most selfish and vain woman I have ever met.'

'Although I hate the thought of her getting her claws into my girls, she has lost the one person on earth she truly cared about.'

'Doesn't it tell you all you need to know that her darling was Lord Edgar Jascombe? I suspect she made him in her own image.'

'Maybe you're right,' she said with a shudder.

'I am doing well.'

'Stop trying to make me laugh, it isn't funny.'

'No, it's not, but a severe bout of the influenza can leave anyone prey to gloomy thoughts and yours must have been severe for Ness to have noticed.'

'I can't stop worrying about them stuck in that stiff old house with the same people who raised their father to be a sly brute.'

'Not even knowing how eager Ness will be to get

them out of the way before his next heir in line is born? I'm sure it won't dare be born a girl, but if it is can you imagine how much worse it would seem to Ness and his heir if there were two other females at Mynham to rub in the fact all their hopes rested with Chert getting it right next time?'

'I have always been surprised the Duke didn't order Lord Chert to marry sooner.'

'Maybe he was waiting for him to meet his match,' Max said, although he suspected Lord Chert had enjoyed being a notable catch too much to pin himself down until his father insisted he marry a suitable future duchess. 'I hope Lady Chert is content to give birth only to boys.'

'She has my sympathy. All *I* want is for my girls to grow up happy in my care instead of the Duke's. Oh, and to be far too wary of charming and heartless men like their father to be taken in by one as I was.'

'It would be better if you showed them how to live fully and freely by example, Georgia love,' he told her and what the devil was he thinking of?

Georgia realised she was gaping at Max with her mouth open and closed it hurriedly. What did he mean live fully and freely? And *love*? It was a careless term of endearment from an old friend, of course, but her heart was still racing—with fear he meant it, not because it sounded like an adventure she would never dare have. And even this far away from him she was tingling with who knew what feeling now and it simply wouldn't *do*.

'What's wrong with how I live?' she said warily.

'You are in danger of living your life through your girls like your mother-in-law did with Jascombe.'

'That's a horrible thing to say.'

'Maybe it is, but you still need to live better than her,' he said implacably.

'I do,' she said shortly.

'You might if you stopped being Jascombe's abused wife, but you haven't yet, have you?'

'Easy for you to say,' she muttered sulkily, but he heard her anyway.

'No, it isn't,' he said grimly and he did look as if it had cost him dear to say it. 'And you never shirked a challenge when we were children,' he added slyly.

'We're not children any more,' she snapped and there was that silly prickle of awareness of him as a man again. It was unaccountable and, as she didn't want to account for it, she ignored it as best she could.

'No,' he said dourly and it was his turn to stare at the hills.

He truly loved this hard-edged but forlorn old place, didn't he? Max had found his own way in life, first at Cambridge as a scholar, then as an unexpected landowner and master of a neglected castle. She could hardly accuse him of not knowing what he was talking about, but she wanted to. She wanted to say he was wrong, yet what *had* she built on the ashes of her supposed-to-be wonderful life when Edgar died? A restless social life to stop her doting on her girls didn't look much of an achievement from here.

Max was rebuilding a castle and estate with fierce energy while she danced and pretended she was carefree in London. He was so much more complicated than he seemed eight years ago, though, wasn't he? This Max was tall instead of lanky and awkward, his face had lost the mismatched look his strong features had as a youth. He had grown into his looks and she imagined him dressed as a fashionable beau and knew he would fascinate the finicky society beauties if he inhabited her world instead of his.

The foundations of her life wanted to shift as jealousy of her fashionable friends ogling him in a rake's dashing clothing insisted he must stay here. She didn't want him to join the charade she had played in for the last five years so maybe he was right and she did need to try harder.

A memory of Max's brother Zachary with his fiery, passionate wife, Martha, both oblivious to anyone else in the midst of a society crush, sneaked into her head and whispered theirs looked a passion worth taking risks for. But she wasn't Martha and why would Max watch her as hungrily as his brother did Martha? She felt herself blush again as curiosity asked how she would feel if he ever did. Hot, she decided, and flustered and she preferred being cool and composed, but she was very glad he was still staring at his beloved hills so he didn't notice that blush and wonder what had caused it.

'Why do you love this place so much?' she asked him once her cheeks felt cool enough to risk it. 'It's not as if you grew up here. If your earliest memories were of creeping around it at night or playing in the grounds with your brother and sisters, I could understand it, but as far as I know you had never set eyes on Holdfast until you came here to see if you would be willing to take it on five years ago.'

'It needed me,' he said with a brooding glance back at the conglomeration of buildings from various periods built inside the castle walls over the years which, along with the original keep, made up an eccentric whole. 'And I needed it,' he added as if honesty demanded it.

'Why?'

'Maybe it was to put my heart and soul into and keep me busy while I drag it back from the edge of ruin and make it a family home again.'

'You don't have a family to make one for,' she said impulsively. 'Oh, I'm so sorry, that was so clumsy of me and so rude,' she added because he might long for a family to fill his lonely old castle with for all she knew.

'I have Becky and my niece now she has asked to live with me,' he said stiffly and didn't seem to want her apology. 'Her sitting rooms and the downstairs are ready for them and now the bedrooms are finished she can move in.'

'That was quick.'

'I was already working on the Little House in case

she and Jack needed a home. He had talked of selling out before Napoleon's escape from Elba and I would have been glad of their help while he decided what he wanted to do next.'

'I am so sorry for your loss as well as your sister's, but why does she want to come here where she'll often be alone while you are so busy? I know your mother asked her to live at Flaxonby Dower House and Zach and his wife begged her to stay at Flaxonby itself. I expect her husband's parents would love to have her and little Phoebe to live with them as well, so why on earth is she coming here instead?'

'Some of us happen to like it, but maybe you should ask her.' Now he sounded offended and he was clearly impatient for her to leave and take her impertinent questions with her.

'Maybe I should, but she would have more company if she lived with your mother or brother or with Captain Sothern's parents,' she persisted because it felt easier to tread on his toes than discuss her sore places again instead.

'Apparently that's why she wants to live here,' Max said stiffly.

'So she can be lonely while you are busy?'

'No, so she can *be* alone when she needs to be and feel the loss of a fine man she truly loved and will miss until her dying day,' he said as if he didn't expect her to understand and he was quite right.

All she had wanted to do when Edgar died was fill the time when her girls didn't need her with as much lightness and gaiety as possible since he had denied her any from the moment they were married.

'You will carry on restoring this place while Becky mourns?'

'It's what she wants.'

Becky had been so jealous of Georgia as a child, because she was the same age as Max and could keep up with him when Becky got left behind—now Becky would have Max all to herself. Georgia supposed living with him really would suit her and Becky could mourn in peace while Max was a loving father figure to his little niece. Georgia was the jealous one now because she would have loved for her girls to have such a good one.

'It sounds like the perfect solution for you both,' she said.

'Aye, we are neither of us very sociable nowadays.'

'Unlike me?'

'Each to their own and Holdfast suits me.'

'You think you are stern and stony and demand respect?' she teased him.

'Not yet, but I do love it and I respect the people who work this land. Holdfast has been my salvation as well as the other way about and I am content here.'

'Are you? Is this really all you ever wanted in life, Max?'

'No,' he said abruptly and frowned as if she had trodden somewhere forbidden. 'I couldn't have that, but Holdfast is more than a second best for a second-best Chilton.'

What couldn't he have, then? Had he loved someone and lost her? The thought of it made her heart
ache, for him of course. Sympathy for a friend
must explain the sick feeling in her belly and this
strange ache in her heart. She didn't want him to
have suffered the same sort of mental anguish she
had endured for a very different reason. Even so, she
couldn't imagine why any young woman with a parti-
cle of sense would turn him down, but someone must
have done for him to look so bleak when he said it.

'You were never second best to Zachary, Max,'
she said gently. 'Your family love you for how you
are and they know you would lay down your life for
any one of them if they ever needed you to.'

He gave her a complicated look, as if she didn't
understand—and he was right, she didn't. 'Do you
feel well enough to walk as far as the church with
me?' he said as if he had been idle with her for long
enough, but was too polite to come out and say so.

'Yes, and I hate to admit that my father-in-law is
right, but your fresh Northumbrian air does seem to
be doing me good,' she told him.

As they walked along side by side, she was relieved the strange tingly feeling had died down. It
must be a leftover symptom from her recent illness
and, of course, it had nothing to do with the fact Max
was so clearly a mature man now instead of the lanky
boy she remembered. It wouldn't do her any good if
he was the cause of it, since he clearly wanted her
gone so he could get on with his real life.

'Good, but I would hate you to think I envy Zach his title and possessions in any way. I got over doing that when my mother told me my father had worked relentlessly to redeem the mortgages on Flaxonby, then tried to make enough money to buy this place back for his mother and she swears the overwork killed him. I always knew Zach had a heavy burden to shoulder when our father died so young and he's always been welcome to Flaxonby and the title as far as I am concerned.'

'Then why call yourself second best?'

He frowned at the distant hills as if measuring words before he said them. She didn't like the idea as she looked back at the ease they once shared and envied her younger self so deeply it felt hurtful.

'Because my grandmother would if she knew I own her precious castle and not Zach,' he said at last. 'She never liked me and maybe that was because I follow my mother's dark looks rather than being a Viking Chilton like Zach. But I do know she would hate the trick Zach and Martha played on Alderman Tolbourne when he gifted them Holdfast because the granddaughter he had disowned as a child had married a viscount.

'When they handed it straight on to me, Lady Margaret DeMayne-Chilton would say they had short-changed her as well as Martha's paternal grandfather. Never mind if Tolbourne only wanted to boast his great-grandson would own the castle of our ancestors one day solely because of his generosity, Lady Margaret would be furious I now own it as well.'

'You are the best owner this place could have and you love it. You are restoring it and she should have been grateful to have two fine grandsons instead of being such an arrogant old killjoy.'

'A compliment, my lady?' he said, but his self-mocking bow set her at a distance again and she felt stupidly bereft.

'Yes, but we are talking about your grandmama,' she prompted him.

'Aye, well, she was the sole heiress to Holdfast in its glory days,' he excused the old dragon, as if loving it had made him understand Lady Margaret better.

'She married the careless rogue who lost it on the turn of a card of her own free will.'

'True,' he admitted with a rueful smile.

'If you accept that Holdfast Castle has the best master it could have, I will think about my frivolous London life a little harder.'

'I will if you will, then,' he said stiffly and her heart ached.

'And I *am* my own woman now,' she said sharply and shrugged to say sorry. 'But thank you for listening to my woes and telling me Lady Chert is with child,' she said to change the subject. 'Now I really must go or it will be dark before I get to Edinburgh and Aunt Isobel will send out a search party.'

They had reached the little church where the family, its servants and estate workers had worshipped for generations.

'We can go back a shorter way,' he said as if he would be delighted to see the back of her so he could return to his labours.

'Good idea.' She suddenly realised why she hardly ever came here—it was because she missed him so much when she left.

'Please give my compliments to your aunt,' he said with chilly politeness as he waited to hand her up into her carriage.

'Of course.' She gave him a slightly mocking curtsy and was shocked when his bow was so slight it was very nearly rude. 'Goodbye, Max,' she said as lightly as she could.

He handed her into her elegant travelling carriage as rapidly as he could, but she felt a stupid bolt of something she didn't want to know about shoot through her at the mere touch of his hand. It felt sharp and hot and shameful and she didn't understand it, or want to. Some of the most handsome gentlemen of the *ton* had handed her into carriages or taken her hand in the dance and she had either felt nothing at all or wanted to snatch her hand away. Now that same hand wanted to linger in Max's and that was just plain ridiculous.

'Goodbye, my lady,' he said austerely.

'Mr Chilton,' she corrected herself and wanted to be glad when he stepped back with an abrupt nod.

She kept her gaze firmly to the front as the coach began to move because she didn't want him to know about the tears in her eyes. At least Aunt Isobel would be pleased to see her. Once Becky was installed at Holdfast, she would be even less welcome here than she had been today. Now all she had to do was learn to put the good bits of the past behind her as well as the bad.

Chapter Four

Max refused to stand and watch Georgia's carriage being driven away like a lovesick boy. He still sighed loudly as he walked away. She had flinched from the touch of his hand on hers while he felt as if it had been shot through with the late Signor Galvani's animal electricity. He was still tingling from the shock and it made him want all the things he could not have yet again.

Confound Georgia for coming here and reawakening old needs and longings he had hoped were dead! He walked wearily back up to the Little House to pack up his tools. It felt as if he had done a hard day's work since Georgia caught him up there instead of a little light carpentry. He would run a nail into his hand or hit his thumb if he tried to use them again today, so he decided to walk off the turmoil that seeing Georgia had left him struggling with rather than risk any more pain.

There wasn't a horse in the stables that was wild

enough to match his mood so he would take a pack and tramp the hills until he was almost himself again. Then he would see about finding a mare his sister could enjoy riding as soon as she felt like it. He knew the exercise and freedom would do her good. It was as well the horse dealers and stablemen didn't know he owned a castle so they wouldn't put up their prices when they knew he was looking for a lady's mount.

Life was so much simpler when it was just him and Sam, his groom, here five years ago. Then they only needed a dry place to sleep and something to eat and drink while Max worked as a labourer to pick up some of the craftsmen's skills to allow him to carry on when the money ran out.

Sam had insisted on getting the most modern of the stable blocks sound, but now Max had almost completed the work on the family living quarters and one or two state rooms and the estate was solvent. A few servants had been added to his payroll to make life more comfortable, but Becky and her baby meant more changes and more servants as well.

Next time Georgia called in passing, he would have a hostess and the correct staff to receive a lady. He could leave Becky to make polite conversation with an old neighbour and stay out of the way. Despite all of his resolutions to forget her, this visit had proved that Georgia could stir up his deepest emotions as no other woman ever had. Now he must stamp off into the hills and work them out of his system.

The new life he had worked so hard to make here felt fragile and finding the right horse for his sister was a good excuse to get away until he had learned how to live with what was instead of what he wanted and could not have again. He would have to walk far and fast to build his dreams back up until his dearest one was of his mythical Mrs Chilton, not the woman he had once loved so deeply, and uselessly, and who had just flinched away from his touch as if he had stung her.

He still felt guilty about being so short with her, deliberately destroying an old friendship that had always felt truly precious, never mind their unequal feelings. It made his fury with the Duke of Ness and his infernal family worse and now he had to get that out of his system as well. He felt raw at the contrast between all he had felt for her over the years and the little she would let herself feel for anyone now.

Once Georgia Welland had been fearless and eager for life and he hated to see the brittle lady of fashion she had become. It also felt as if she had scraped a wound he had fooled himself was healed, but now was raw and aching.

Ness was a bungling idiot! Max struggled to think past his fury as he threw necessities into a pack. How could the old windbag have left Georgia thinking she could lose her children? Max would put good money on the pompous old fool being overjoyed if Georgia remarried so he could pass guardianship of his granddaughters over to her new husband and wash his hands of them.

Why hadn't he told her that Lady Chert was with child so that he wanted Georgia properly fit to take her children off his hands again? He supposed Ness didn't think lesser people had any feelings and in his eyes Georgia would always be less since she wasn't born in a nobleman's bed.

It had always puzzled him why Ness let Jascombe marry an innocent debutante without a powerful family to protect her, but light dawned at last. Ness had let his repellent second son marry beneath him to make sure that his precious line went on, even if his direct heir didn't secure it. Max felt furious with himself for not working it out when he rode away from Mynham on that bleak winter morning five years ago.

Bile rose in his throat as he realised Ness had told Jascombe to marry a cit's daughter deliberately, to make sure Lord Edgar's sins didn't come out in a court or end up being discussed over tea and scandal by the tabbies related to his unlucky bride. The shabby truth was that Ness had let Lord Edgar marry Georgia *because* her father lacked rank and influence.

Mr Welland would not have been able to fight for his daughter's well-being and happiness even if she had told him about Lord Edgar's vicious pleasures. But she knew that, didn't she? Max's hands balled into fists, but he had to force them open again because Ness was well over sixty and Jascombe was dead and there was nobody left to hit. The violence and abuse Georgia had had to endure just because Ness wanted a fallback heir if his precious eldest son failed to produce one made the old sick fury kick in his belly.

He had thrown his outrage and pity for her into undoing the damage another heartless fool had done to Holdfast five years ago. He recalled the feel of Georgia sobbing in his arms and being so helpless to put things right for her and had to unclench his fists yet again. He absently rubbed the familiar ache above his heart, but of course it was for an old friend this time, not for a lover he was never going to have.

Georgia was safe now and he had wasted enough frustrated passion on her. It wasn't her fault, but seeing her again had made him realise he had gone on dreaming about her behind his own back, as if the besotted boy who fell in love with her eight years ago was still insisting he could love no other. The boy was wrong; he had to be.

If Max dragged this trip out long enough, Becky might be here when he got back and they could begin a new life here. His sister would happily stand between Max and her childhood enemy if Georgia did call on her way home. He was so tired of wanting and not having that he was going to let her.

'Brother, dearest,' Becky greeted Max with a gallant smile ten days later when he led the sturdy mare he knew would carry her all day into the stable yard.

His heart lifted at the sight of his little sister waiting for him and looking more like her old self already.

'Welcome home, Sister, dear,' he said and threw the reins at his grinning groom so he could hug her properly. 'I'm so glad that you're here, Becky love, and so very sorry I wasn't here when you arrived.'

'I'm so glad to be here, too, Max, but you stink and you look as if you haven't shaved for a week.'

'I haven't, but it took a lot longer to find a horse to suit you than I thought it would. I hope she meets your high standards now we are here?'

'Yes, she's lovely. You have kind eyes, don't you, darling?' Becky said as she petted the mare and Max could see they had bonded straight away so at least he had got something right.

'Sam tells me you had a fashionable visitor on the day you took off on your mission to find this sweetheart for me in such a hurry,' Becky said almost casually. 'Whatever was Lady Edgar Jascombe doing in the wilds of Northumberland?'

'It's not that wild and she called to pass on her parents' good wishes,' he lied.

'Hasn't she heard of writing paper and ink?'

'Oh, come now, Rebecca, you know as well as I do that Lady Edgar and I are not related in any way so she cannot write to me without causing comment.'

Becky's unladylike snort said she didn't believe propriety would matter if Georgia wanted to write to him badly enough. She clearly didn't know Georgia was no longer the impulsive girl she remembered and he supposed they didn't move in the same circles nowadays so why would she?

'Even if she doesn't want you, she would hate for another woman to steal you away.'

'I know you don't like her because we used to leave you behind as children, but that was my fault. You are my little sister and I should have waited for you. Georgia just wanted my advice on a family matter and maybe you should give her the benefit of the doubt.'

'Why? I know it wasn't as simple as friendship for you back then. I doubt if it is now if the truth be told, although I hope I'm wrong,' Becky told him and there was too much genuine concern in her eyes for him to be offended. 'I know she hurt you when she was the belle of local society and everyone else thought you were only a boy,' she went on. 'Don't pretend I'm imagining things, because I always knew you better than you wanted me to.

'I hated the way you closed in on yourself after that beating you took in London when you insisted on going there because your precious Georgia was having her debut. No, don't shake your head and pretend I don't know what I'm talking about, Max. I knew she had hurt you when you came home so sad and silent. Lord Edgar arranged for that attack to get you out of his way, didn't he?'

'Why on earth would you think so, Becky?' he said, shocked she was so perceptive. He had only seen the sly purpose behind that attack after Georgia had told him what a hell her marriage had been. He had put two and two together and made four then because he hated the sneering devil so much it was easy to think the worst of him.

'Although she used to let you trail around after her like a puppy, there was always a risk she might realise you are a far better man than her precious Lord Edgar would ever have been,' Becky replied and he held up a hand—whether it was to stop her or concede defeat even he didn't know.

'You are more perceptive than I was,' he said bleakly.

'I wasn't in love with her. Lord Edgar must have thought you were a threat to want you out of the way,' she said as if she thought he needed comforting for his youthful folly. He just wished she would let sleeping dogs lie.

'Sometimes you terrify me, Little Sister.'

'You are only calling me that to stop me trying to find out what she's done to you this time. I want you to be free of her and happy with someone kinder so, please, let her go now, Max. Maybe even for her sake as well as for your own.'

'She has nobody else to confide in.'

'Then she should stand on her own two feet or find someone else to keep her secrets for her. She must need real friends or a new lord to marry by now.'

He could hardly accuse his sister of not understanding what she was talking about when she was still reeling from losing her husband in battle, but he couldn't break Georgia's confidence and tell Becky why that was never going to happen.

'I should have remembered how ruthlessly truthful you are when I invited you to live here for as long as you liked,' he joked. 'I can't help wondering why I was so keen when you are already taking over my life and you have only just got here.'

'Because you love me and I love you and you have lived alone for too long. I don't want to be pitied at every turn, or told time will heal when I don't want it to. I don't want to forget Jack as everybody else seems to think I should: he was the love of my life.

'Now, please will you take this sweetheart to her new stable and get her settled for me while I find my hungry little horror before she wakes up and makes her nanny come to find me. Remember, I only interfere because I love you and want the best for you,' she said hastily and threw the reins back at him before dashing away to find her baby.

Little Phoebe wasn't even six months old yet, so of course Becky had to rush off to nurse her. The pity of their situation hit all over again—why did the innocent have to suffer most for this peace the country was finally able to enjoy at such terrible cost?

At least his littlest niece was too young to know she was fatherless now and that was even more reason to make her childhood as secure and happy as he could without Jack Sothern to adore his daughter alongside Becky. His sister was brave enough to start a new life, so it was time he was, too. He would search for a wife as soon as Becky had settled in and her deepest mourning period was over. Until then he had plenty of work to do.

A fortnight after her visit to Holdfast Georgia waved goodbye to Aunt Isobel and her burly, prosperous sons and fine tribe of grandchildren. She felt much better and far more optimistic after being so royally entertained, as if it was their duty to make sure she went back to the Sassenach south in a healthier state than she left it, if she really must go back there.

She had gained a little weight and hadn't coughed for several days. If she went to Mynham, even the Duke would have to admit she was much improved. He might even agree that spending the rest of the summer at a sleepy seaside resort with her daughters was the best cure for any remaining weakness and that he need not worry about them again until Millie was ready to be presented at Court.

She was still waving at her aunt and her family when the coach trundled down the street and they were finally lost to view. Out on the road to Riverdale first and then onwards to retrieve her daughters, Georgia wondered what Max was doing now. Had Becky got to Holdfast yet and what had she said when she found out Georgia was there a fortnight ago? It didn't matter what Becky thought, though, did it?

Max was part of Georgia's past, judging by the cool send-off he gave her two weeks ago. Never mind, her girls were all that mattered now and she had slept a lot better since telling Max her woes and realising he was quite right—the Duke had no time for girls so why would he keep hers?

Thank goodness Max had told her the Duke had a potential grandson on the way. He was probably right to urge her to think harder about how her life ran as well. If it was the last piece of advice he ever gave her, at least it was good. Her London life seemed idle and tedious now she had been made to step away from it and weigh up the alternatives.

She didn't want to keep thinking about Max, but somehow she couldn't seem to help herself. She shifted restlessly against the squabs and stared out of the window as if the landscape was fascinating because she knew he didn't want her to dwell on him

He would look like a fine son-in-law to Mrs Welland now he had a castle and estate to add to his noble birth. Maybe she would send him warning to stay away from his old home when she was on her way north next time. She squirmed at the thought of her mother's grand social ambitions for her even now and it was one good reason not to bring the girls to Riverdale to enjoy the same carefree childhood she had.

Her parents loved her and she loved them, but she didn't want her girls growing up thinking that rank mattered more than a man's character. She had when she made her debut; Edgar's birth and practised charm and his apparent devotion to her had made her forget that she grew up with a much better man than he would ever be, even if Max was a boy then.

There, she was thinking about Max again! She didn't want a man in her life, not even if it was him and that was very unlikely. She reached for the Parisian fashion plates Huggins had sent for so they could consider how to update her winter wardrobe. Georgia tried to take a proper interest in what to wear during the Little Season and which extremes of fashion were a step too far even for a sophisticated widow like her. Paris and even London seemed so far away it felt ridiculous to order yet more impractical clothes to add to the ones she already had.

Huggins would be so shocked if she ordered a countrywoman's sensible attire instead of impractical fabrics made up in frivolous styles and covered in all sorts of luxurious trimmings she wasn't sure she liked the look of. Georgia wondered why that practical wardrobe didn't seem such a silly idea as it would have done before she was ill. Hmm, maybe it really was time she reconsidered the way she lived now and made a few changes.

Chapter Five

It took Georgia an endless half-hour after arriving at her parents' home to escape her mother's fussing for an unloved corner of the house where she could reread the first of the letters waiting for her. She hadn't heard a word of the local gossip her mother had recounted while pressing tea and delicacies on her pale and silent daughter after the journey north she insisted had done Georgia no good at all, just as she predicted.

What a good thing she had had so much practice at hiding her feelings, Georgia decided with a heavy sigh. She could not have endured her mother's exclamations and questions if she had let out the gasp of horror she wanted to on first reading the Duke's tirade.

It began brusquely and launched into angry complaint without more ado.

Daughter-in-law,
Your daughters are wilful, disobedient and

wicked. They have been intent on causing as much trouble as possible for their elders since they got here, but this is the final straw.

I am astonished that you have done so little to correct their stubborn, defiant natures. You have indulged their every whim beyond all reason and they will grow up monstrous and pettish and a disgrace to their illustrious family name if I do not intervene.

I shall make sure they are disciplined as they so clearly need to be from this moment on.

She stopped reading and took a deep breath to stop herself shouting her fury aloud. He was so wrong; Millie and Helen had inherited none of Edgar's meanness of spirit and she had always made sure they had good principles to live up to. Her first impulse was to order her carriage and tear down south to confront him, but she must think this through first.

The Duke was the girls' guardian so she needed to get them away from the pompous old fool and ensure her children didn't grow up enduring the stern regime he had outlined. He would expect them to be quiet and obedient and crushed and the Duchess would do her best to pet and spoil them behind his back. She paced the awkward room, knowing all that mattered was that her girls were loved and listened to and never mind having self-important idiots as their paternal grandparents.

*After upsetting their grandmother so much
she has suffered a nervous collapse they had
the effrontery to run away. From Mynham, of
all places!*

The horrible letter went on as if he thought it was
a paradise on earth. Given how dangerous this bad
old world was for lone children, she hated the idea of
them alone in it, so why didn't he share her terror?

*Your daughters feigned sleep, then dressed
and crept down the backstairs to stow away in
one of the carts taking newly harvested grain
to Mynham Magna for milling.*
*They were only found when the carters
reached the mill, so there was no hope of hiding their appalling conduct. They even told
the miller's wife they meant to keep hiding in
carts and on barges until they got to Yorkshire
to find their mother.*
*Half the neighbourhood know my grand-
daughters had the effrontery to run away from
one of the finest houses in the land by now and
all sorts of unsavoury gossip must be doing
the rounds.*

Ah, at last—there was the truth of the matter.
The girls' escape was public knowledge so there
would be speculation about how they were treated
to make them want to run away. That insight made

her certain the Duke would not take this back and she read on with a heavy heart.

> *I cannot countenance my grandchildren be-*
> *having with such ingratitude ever again, so*
> *they will remain here for good. I shall super-*
> *vise their education and make sure they learn*
> *to conduct themselves as aristocratic young*
> *ladies should.*
>
> *Unless you marry a sensible man, whom I*
> *can trust to make sure my granddaughters do*
> *not bring disgrace on their illustrious family*
> *name ever again, they will remain at Mynham*
> *until they are old enough to marry.*
>
> *If you choose to return here your former*
> *apartments are unoccupied, but I shall ex-*
> *pect you to take your role as the mother of my*
> *granddaughters seriously.*
>
> *They, and you, need to remember what is*
> *due to my illustrious family name and lofty*
> *position and conduct yourselves as true la-*
> *dies from now on.*

The brass-faced cheek of the man. He knew Edgar was a devious and violent man, but of course *he* had kept his sins a secret. The injustice of it, the sheer hypocrisy of her father-in-law's reasoning, or lack of it, was breathtaking. Millie and Helen had run away from him and his stupid Duchess, for good-ness sake! That didn't seem to cause him anxiety and now he was going to insist that her girls grow up in that awful old barrack. She had to free them from the chains Edgar had put on them by taking one last swipe at his wife from beyond the grave.

With the uncomfortable fact that Ness *was* their legal guardian nagging at her, she took a few deep breaths and opened the second letter.

Leonora thought the Duke would reconsider when he had calmed down enough to listen to reason, did she? Georgia wasn't hopeful but was still glad Leonora had written, too. Why wasn't she surprised the whole wretched business began with the Duchess losing her temper? This time it was because Millie and Helen didn't want to stay indoors and be petted like lapdogs, so they escaped into the grounds to avoid her.

> *Unfortunately the Duchess was too busy flying into a rage and having hysterics to tell me they were missing. She ordered me to free them from their afternoon lessons, so I didn't know they were gone until they came back hungry and grubby.*
>
> *The Duchess demanded I whip them and, when I refused, threatened me with dismissal and told the girls they were a disgrace to their father's memory. She said she would make sure they never saw you again, nor were allowed to write to you. She added a wish that you had been the one who died five years ago instead and hoped the influenza would carry you off.*

> *When the girls became hysterical she re-*
> *tired to bed with the headache.*

Georgia loathed the selfish woman for making her girls cry, and for making them think they needed to steal out of the house in the dark to find out if their mama was alive or not. She hated the thought of them creeping out like that. Their busy day must have meant they were so weary the rocking of the carts lulled them to sleep so that was why nobody heard a thing until they halted at the mill. Even when they were brought back and should have been hugged and comforted, their ordeal wasn't over.

Leonora wrote that the Duke had raged at them and the Duchess made no mention of what happened earlier.

> *His Grace says he is taking charge of their*
> *upbringing and gave orders that Nanny was*
> *to be locked in the night nursery with them so*
> *they can never run away again.*

The letter ended with a scrawled signature and Georgia was glad Leonora had no time to offer her any more false hope. She would have to go and live at Mynham as well, but the tension between her and the Duchess would be nigh unbearable this time.

She discovered she had stopped pacing and was sitting in a stiff old chair and rocking back and forth for comfort, but it wasn't working. She felt so desolate it made her remember how wonderfully safe she had felt in Max's arms five years ago and wished he was here now, but she should think about her girls, not her own lack of a nice broad shoulder to lean on.

She couldn't tell her parents why she was so anxious about her children under the ducal roof when the Duke would crush Papa like an annoying fly if he fought for custody of his granddaughters. The Duke had so much power and influence he could ride roughshod over a man even his own wife called a cit so she couldn't drag her father into this.

Max was the only person who could understand why she was distraught about her children having to live at Mynham until they were grown and she could hardly go to Holdfast and tell him. He had made it clear he had his own life now and there wasn't any room in it for her. She didn't blame him; he had Becky and her baby to provide a home for but, oh, how she envied that little girl Max's love and care on her daughters' behalf.

As she sat, feeling so alone with her worries, it was hard not to yearn for him. It had felt like a return to warmth and sanity and hope when Max held her five years ago. She had stolen out of a house in mourning after a sleepless night, thinking it had been a mistake to pass him that note and meaning to say she had only wanted him to send her best wishes to her family and friends at home. Then she saw him waiting for her in a chilly and unloved corner of Mynham Woods and the story of her miserable marriage came tumbling out as if his very presence demanded honesty.

If only she could marry Max, he would take responsibility for her girls and the Duke would happily wash his hands of them all. It was a ridiculous idea, but a sneaky inner voice whispered it would solve all her problems in one go, if only he would agree.

He wouldn't *want* to marry her. He knew the true state of her marriage to Edgar and that she never wanted to be touched like that again. Max was so stiff and formal when they parted two weeks ago, so impatient to get on with his busy life at Holdfast, she knew he would hate the very idea, but the Duke's furious letter proved her worries were justified.

Max might take pity on her daughters and agree to marry their mother to set them free. It was asking too much of an old friend, but what if she didn't try? She would never forgive herself if she let even the sliver of a chance he might do such a huge thing for the sake of her girls pass her by. The Duke could send them to the strictest school he could find if she gave in and he still didn't think their lives were harsh enough.

She unclenched her fists because being furious and frustrated with the Duke would not do her any good. She would think about Max instead since he didn't make her want to shoot him in cold blood and she wouldn't be much use to her daughters if she was hung for murder.

Until two weeks ago she had thought of Max as

the boy he had still seemed five years ago, but he was the only man she would ever trust after Edgar had shown her one could be charming and urbane on the outside and so wicked inside she felt a fool for not seeing it. A white marriage with Max would change everything and she knew she could trust him not to force his repellent needs on her and keep her children safe.

Desperation outran the feeling that it wouldn't be fair to even ask him to marry her. Max might agree to make such a huge sacrifice for Millie and Helen's sake, because he was a good man. They could live at Holdfast for a while, then pretend she could not endure the country so they would live apart for most of the year. She could spend a few weeks in Northumberland now and again and he would spare her a week or so to keep up appearances in London.

It *was* a last desperate throw of the dice and it probably wouldn't work, but she had to try. She would be an apology for a mother if she didn't do all she could to avoid her girls having to live at Mynham for good.

'No! Absolutely not,' Max barked out his outrage and paced the sparsely furnished drawing room like a caged tiger.

He looked as if he wanted to put a few hundred miles between them instead of yards. Georgia would have to go to Mynham and accept her fate. The idea of living in the same rooms where Edgar used to belittle and abuse her felt so desolate that she had one last try at persuading Max it was a good idea.

'It would only be until my girls are old enough to wed. Then you could start a new life and you would still be young enough to begin again,' she pleaded. 'If I pay him enough I'm sure a hired man will agree to run off with me so you can sue him, divorce me and marry again.'

'After you have proved so publicly that you don't want me? What sort of cold-blooded saint do you think I am, Georgia? I'm *not* a eunuch. I couldn't marry you and not want you as a husband wants his wife. I would go mad or have to beg for my release from purgatory before the year was out.'

'Oh, I see,' she said and felt a fool for thinking a white marriage was even possible for such a vigorous and masculine man. He was probably too honourable to take a mistress as well and her wonderful plan looked ridiculous even to her as she stared at his broad back.

'Do you really think me such an apology for a man that you could use me as cover, then throw me aside when you didn't need me any more?' he demanded furiously.

'No, that's not what I meant at all,' she argued, even if it was. 'You are a fine, mature man and a great many women would be deeply honoured to be your wife,' she said clumsily.

'Just not you,' he said flatly and sounded so sternly

remote she shivered and realised how cold her life was going to be without even a trace of him in it.

'I'm not normal, not marriageable,' she argued wildly and it was true.

He frowned even more fiercely and marched away from her with his fists clenched as if he wanted to hit something, hard. With his back turned again she risked a wobbly smile because it would be a wall or door and he would only end up hurting himself.

'And you are, Max,' she persisted. 'All the local beauties must sigh in unison when you stroll into one of their drawing rooms and make their beaux look like old men or silly boys,' she added and he swung round with an even fiercer frown on his sternly handsome face. 'I expect they dream of marrying you every night and their suitors curse you for being so much more desirable than they are,' she persisted even so.

'Miss Welland never desired me and nor does Lady Edgar Jascombe,' he said wearily. The coldness in his usually warm brown eyes made her feel as if she was standing on an ice floe and might never be warm again.

'Miss Welland had all the wrong dreams, but this is reality,' she argued.

'You dreamt of marrying a title and fine old lineage and I was not good enough for you back then, my lady. I had nothing but my patrimony and place at Cambridge in those days, but does your mother think I will *do* now I have a half-repaired castle and a once-grand estate?'

'Mama doesn't know I need a husband and please don't be so bitter, Max. I would never have asked you to do such a monstrous thing for me if I wasn't so desperate to get my girls back,' she said and barely managed to bite back a groan when the words came out of her mouth and sounded so inept even to her.

'Desperate?' He sounded even more bitterly offended now as he paced up and down the grand old room before he was calm enough to carry on. 'I might be honoured by your gracious proposal when I calm down and take in its true quality,' he told her at last.

'Stop being so sarcastic; I didn't mean to make a botch of things. I am nervous and there *is* no right way to ask what I just asked you to do for me, but I'm sorry I was so clumsy. I found the Duke's letter when I got back from Edinburgh and panicked, thought of you and dashed straight here. I was a fool to even think it would be a good way out and it's too late to mend our friendship, but please forgive me for abusing it so badly.'

He was silent for so long that tears pricked her eyes as she mourned a common past she had ground into the dust. He marched across the room to stare out of one of the newly leaded windows and kept his back to her as if he was beyond words and beyond even looking at her. She turned to go, but it felt cowardly to sneak away, so she stared at his rigid back and searched for better words. She had to make their final parting feel better before she went off to begin a new life so horribly tainted by the old one.

'I shall live at Mynham so I can make sure the Duchess doesn't take over Millie and Helen's lives as she did Edgar's,' she told the back of his head. 'I expect the Duke will leave us to get on with our lives in peace if I manage to keep them quiet and out of his way, just as Edgar was kept quiet as a son the Duke had no time for when *he* was young.'

'You feel sorry for Jascombe because his own father didn't like him, don't you? How can you after what he did to you?' Max said, as if this only made her insulting offer worse and he still wouldn't look at her.

'Not for the man he grew into, but for the boy whose father ignored him because he already had an heir and didn't have any love left over for a spare? Yes, I pity him that much. The Duke did as much damage by ignoring him as the Duchess did in spoiling him beyond all reason and refusing to correct his misdeeds while hiding them from his father.'

'Excuse me from sharing your compassion.'

'You don't need to pity him, though, do you? You don't have to try to understand what made him a secret monster the moment he got his ring on my finger and I was his to do whatever he pleased to under the fine old laws of our land, but I do, Max. I paid for what they did to that boy and they bent him so far out of shape I have no idea what he would have been like if he was raised as a boy should be.

'Neither of his parents cared what trying to please a father who couldn't be pleased and a mother who was never *dis*pleased would do to him. I care how my daughters fit into the world because I'm their mother and I can't let them grow up thinking their hopes and fears are more important than anyone else's.'

'If they enjoyed being petted by the Duchess, they would never have run away to find you when she frightened them. It sounds as if they are more like you than their father and already have minds of their own.'

She felt a little bit complimented that Max thought them being like her was a good thing after he had refused her plea with such furious contempt, but she wasn't about to let it go to her head.

'Their governess sounds capable of teaching them where the line between right and wrong lies so I don't see why you must live at Mynham. It's close enough to London to visit them regularly and still lead your own life,' he argued as if he was trying to convince himself.

'The Duchess can get rid of a governess and I must be at Mynham to make sure my girls know they are loved. I can't pretend my daughters are of no importance until they are old enough to be presented and I would be a coward to let living at Mynham again stop me caring for my daughters.'

'You will live in the same place you endured three years of unholy and miserable matrimony with Jascombe, then?'

'Yes, I have had five years of freedom and it won't be for ever.'

It will just feel like it, she added silently.

'Until your girls are of age or marry.' He turned to face her again with such a bleak look in his dark eyes she almost wished he hadn't.

'We will live as normally as it is possible to in such a grand and self-important place,' she said with a wanting-to-be-careless shrug.

'They should grow up happy and expecting the best when it's their turn to marry.'

'Any mother would want that for them, but I was both as a child and thought I would be happy with Lord Edgar Jascombe—look how wrong I was,' she said and heard the beginnings of hysteria in her own voice. She took a deep breath and fought it. 'At least I will look hard at their suitors when the time comes,' she added as lightly as she could to let him know she wasn't going to tip over the edge and embarrass him.

'If they watched you being happy first, they might be more demanding when it came to making their own choice of husband. You did say the Duke offered to hand guardianship over to your next husband so you could live wherever you chose to if you married again.'

She knew Max wasn't a cruel man, so why was he reminding her of impossible things? 'No, I could live where my husband chose,' she argued bitterly.

'Have you tried to find a man you could trust since Jascombe died?'

'No, why would I?' she snapped, furious he even

thought she should overcome her shame at asking him to marry her and being brusquely refused.

'Because you are lonely and have two wilful daughters to bring up?' he said almost gently, but why was he pointing out the painfully obvious?

'I'm not lonely and being their mother is a pleasure, not a duty,' she argued although she was lying and would feel even more alone at Mynham now.

At least last time Max was still her friend and might have thought kindly of her when he looked up from his studies or ran for a lecture at Cambridge. The fact he wasn't her friend any more hurt more than it had when she drove away from here two weeks ago. He probably hated her now, but at least on the way back to Riverdale nobody would see her cry about it, since she left in such a hurry that Huggins was still there.

'You proved that you don't like your own company when you moved to Mayfair,' Max argued as coolly as if she was a stranger and she supposed she must get used to it.

'I spent three years watching every move I made for mistakes Edgar could punish me for later and I felt old and cold and weary, so I wanted to feel young again. I wanted to be easy in my own skin and he was no longer able to forbid every pleasure in life,' she told him. 'And I *needed* not to dote on my children as the Duchess did on Edgar. I want them to grow up happy and independent and living in London, being busy doing nothing much, stopped me spoiling them. You think I lived a shallow, pointless life, but I didn't want to fill the blank spaces by clinging to my children and they need to know a woman doesn't need a man to make her happy.'

'And are you?'

'Am I what?'

'Happy.'

'None of us was scared so, yes, I was as happy as most women are if they don't have to worry about a roof over their heads or food and warm clothes for their children.'

'Is that happiness or freedom from want?'

'It would look like bliss to those not as lucky as I am,' she argued.

'Once they were used to being warm and fed they might expect more from life and so should you. You are six and twenty, Georgia. There should be more to life for you than mere existence, like happiness and fulfilment and even love if you are lucky.'

'It's just an illusion,' she said dismissively.

'You expected so much from life when we were young,' he said with a shake of his dark head as if her being so set against wanting very much from it now made him sad.

'I had a head full of dreams that turned to nightmares.'

'That doesn't mean you have to stop dreaming,' he said as if he thought she should put herself on the marriage mart. Why couldn't he see it was impossible?

'I live in the real world,' she argued even as she felt the loss of the ardent young lovers *they* could have been with an ache in her heart that might never fade now she had let herself feel it too late.

'I don't like the look of it, then.' His frown darkened as he stared at her even more broodingly, then seemed to make up his mind. 'Do you trust me, Georgia?' he asked abruptly.

'More than I do myself,' she said truthfully and met his gaze with a tiny spark of hope alive again when it probably had no right to be. She would let him make such a huge sacrifice if he had changed his mind. She *was* that selfish. And she needed her girls to be safe from the damage the Jascombes did to spare children so much it overcame all scruples.

'Why?'

'Because you never bullied or tried to intimidate me as a boy and you care about people,' she said. 'And you have always treated me as an equal although you are the son of a viscount and my grandfather Welland was a cit and most of your kind feel free to look down on us.'

'How can you be so sure I haven't changed since we were children?'

'Are you trying to tell me your character turned inside out after we ran wild together as children?'

'Probably not,' Max admitted with a sigh and he didn't look very pleased about it.

'Then you still have a good heart and the strength not to lash out in a temper when you don't get your own way. You look after your family and you made a home here for Becky when she needed one.'

'What a short list of good qualities you do demand of a husband, Lady Edgar.'

'No, you are my friend and I know you too well to ask for more.'

'Aye, and there lies the rub,' she thought she heard him murmur. 'You need to listen to my terms if you really think you want to marry me,' he cautioned her out loud and her small glimmer of hope threatened to blaze out of control.

'Very well,' she agreed meekly, thinking they had to be better than the Duke of Ness's demand she live under his roof with her daughters or take no part in their upbringing.

'The only one that's important is we would marry on a promise to strive for it to be a real marriage eventually. You would have to agree to at least try to trust me to be your true husband one day. That's the only way I could make you such important vows before God and my family, Georgia. I can't perjure myself and not mean to honour every one so that's the only way I can marry you. Call it a promise to mean your vows to me one day if you like, but know that I won't change my mind. I can't give you a white marriage until you don't need me any longer, then tamely stand aside while you run off with another man.'

Chapter Six

Georgia gasped with shock at his changes to her plan for a marriage in name only and shook her head in frantic denial. 'No!' she exclaimed with horror and backed away from the vigorous masculine fact of him in a haze of panic.

'No,' she repeated and wondered where her wits had gone to stand here and listen to him with her mouth open like a stock fish and her gaze fixed on his sternly handsome face as he blasted her hopes to powder. 'I can't do that thing ever again. Not with any man, not even you,' she whispered and put her hand to her mouth to stop it trembling at the very thought of enduring the marital bed again, even with the only man she could trust not to hurt her.

'I wouldn't expect you to be my true wife at the outset, Georgia,' he told her more gently and raised his hand as if he wanted to take hers and comfort her, but dropped it back to his side when she backed away again.

'I'm not a brute. I won't demand what you can't freely give me. You would have to learn to trust me with your head *and* your heart before we were truly man and wife and I promise never to lay a finger on you in anger. I would rather cut my hand off than hurt you with it. I could drag that rat you married out of his grave and beat his corpse until it was sorry for what he did to you, but I'm not a violent man, I promise.'

'I know you're not,' she said and it was true. But the act of so-called love made her flinch from the thought of coupling even with him one day, regardless of the stupid little jitters deep inside when she walked through the gardens with him a couple of weeks ago. They would never outshine the memory of how it felt to be taken whenever her husband felt like it.

How could she promise to love, honour and obey Max for the rest of her natural life when Edgar made her the same promises and broke every single one? She wasn't the pristine and loving young wife Max should marry and enjoy a joyous wedding night with.

'In your head you know it,' he argued as if he understood her better than she did herself. 'Deep down, where Jascombe hurt and humiliated you the most I don't think you don't trust anyone. Because of him you have no idea how it feels to truly make love, Georgia, and if you don't even want to yearn for me as your lover and match me kiss for kiss one day, then don't marry me.

'I can only wed you on the hope lovemaking will eventually bind us for life and leave no room for the ifs and buts and maybes I can see forming in your busy mind. I can't marry you for any less than a promise to at least try to mean our vows. I certainly won't endure the devil's bargain you have just insulted us both with, Georgiana.'

She wished he wouldn't call her by the full version of her name when it sounded so stiff and formal on his lips. She knew he was trying to distance himself from her again. He obviously didn't think she had enough courage to risk his version of marriage, but there *was* still a tiny little snag of something curious and forbidden at the heart of her whispering *maybe*. If they *did* marry on his terms she would have to strive for so much she hadn't even wanted to think about. But he was Max. She couldn't fear *him*, even if the very idea of such intimacy made her sick with nerves.

'You would have to agree to take at least half of my fortune for your own use if we marry and try to keep those promises, Max. I can't let you sacrifice everything you are for me and give nothing in return. I may never be able to make love with you, so there are many more risks on your side than there are on mine. Because of that I must be able to give you something back and you could do so much good with it here.'

'I don't want your money,' he said as if the very idea revolted him and he had to pace again.

'You may not, but your tenants and your castle

certainly do. However hard you work, it will take decades to get the estate properly back to normal. Parts of your castle that you haven't been able to rebuild yet should at least be repaired before they fall down if you won't be sensible.'

'Sensible? I can provide for my family, thank you very much,' he said with so much pride she nearly smiled. He thought he was such a humble man it was almost funny.

'Of course you can, but, speaking for myself, I prefer you alive instead of following your father to an early grave from hard work.'

He shrugged, but she could tell by his sudden stiffness her words had hit home. He had grown up without a father and would not want that for any child they might have and what a heart-racing, panicky idea that was. Maybe she could just think of her own daughters and Becky's little girl instead for now.

'I need to think a lot harder about this; we both do,' he said as if her condition was almost as hard for him as his was for her.

'True,' she said. If they risked it, this would be a very different kind of marriage to the one she had come here to ask for and it did need a lot more thinking about.

'I might as well return to Yorkshire with you so we can resolve it there instead of miles apart. We will need to relearn each other as adults if we are to even be friends again, Georgia, let alone lovers. And stop panicking; I will give you time.'

'Thank you,' she said. Planning a journey back to their respective childhood homes with such a huge decision hanging over their heads felt very odd somehow. 'We had best get on with it, I suppose.'

'We had best get there before dark so we don't have to marry anyway to save your reputation,' he agreed with a weary smile.

'It's not that far and there is supposed to be a moon tonight,' she almost argued, but Becky might decide to poison her tea if she stayed here much longer and Max might think better of the whole idea and she really didn't want him to do that.

'What do you want to do next?' Georgia said early the next morning. Max was waiting where they had always met up for their childhood adventures. She had asked him that question so often when they were young, but they weren't children now and her entire future might depend on his reply.

'Let's walk,' he said and waited for her to lead the way.

It felt so odd recalling how headlong and busy they were about their adventures once upon a time as they strolled along the edges of her father's fish pond and out into Max's brother's parkland, on the path the villagers used as a short cut to get to work at Flaxonby. Once they knew every foot of both estates, but it felt so different now they were grown up and had lived away from here for so long, it felt like another lifetime.

'I had to sneak out before Huggins came in and tried to chivvy me into something totally unsuitable for a proper walk in the country,' she said, more for something to say than because she thought he was interested in fashion, or her lack of it this morning. 'I was amazed to find this old gown still fits me.'

'It suits you, it always did,' he said distractedly.

'And did you steal those fine clothes from your brother's wardrobe?' she teased him. 'You certainly won't be able to wear any of *your* old clothes now you have developed more muscles than a prize-fighter.'

'And I wonder you are so slender after carrying two children. Joan is always complaining hers have ruined her girlish figure.'

'Your elder sister has had four more of them than I have and I am thinner than I usually am at the moment.'

'Because of the influenza that caused all this trouble in the first place?' he asked and looked a little harder at her, as if he suspected she would fade away if he didn't keep a close eye on her.

'And the worry,' she admitted with a shrug. 'I'm usually as healthy as a horse, although I never thought that a very good comparison when some of them have such delicate constitutions and suffer all sorts of unfortunate ailments.'

Now she was making conversation as if they were nodding acquaintances. Maybe he thought so too, since he didn't even make one of those *humph?* noises men used to ward off polite conversation. They both knew she was trying to avoid the more difficult one they must have as they walked on in silence. He was indulging her, she decided, and was slightly offended.

'What *do* you want to do next, then?' she repeated her first question since he hadn't answered it.

'Are you prepared to at least try to be my wife in every sense of the word one day, Georgia?' he countered her question with his very serious one and she couldn't read his thoughts at all to see how he wanted her to reply, the tricky wretch.

'Yes,' she said at last and hoped he knew just saying the word had used up all the bravery she had.

'I would feel better if you did not look as if you have been condemned to the guillotine.'

'I'm sorry, Max. I'm nervous and I promise you nobody will know we are not the perfect couple when we are together in public if you do decide to marry me.'

'I'm sure they won't,' he said, all the acting she had to do while she was married to Edgar bleak in his gaze as he met hers.

It felt as if Edgar's sly ghost was sitting in an oak tree nearby like a malicious spirit, wishing them all the bad luck in the world, so she met Max's eyes as bravely as she could and refused to listen to it.

'I won't have to act confidence with you, Max, because you have always given it to me. I won't need to pretend I am at ease with you since we were always easy together when we ran wild over this land and my father's as children.'

'You won't feel at ease with me now we are full

grown, though, will you? Not with the promises we are going to make to one another keeping you on edge and you expecting me to pounce on you like a hungry wolf at any moment,' he said as if he doubted this was a good idea deep down.

Even if she shared those doubts and that fear she could not turn her back on this chance to be so much more to one another than they were now. She had to think about the happiness of her daughters in the here and now as well.

'I know you too well to do that and I shall learn to be braver in time,' she said and hoped it was true.

'Love can't be forced, Georgia. I won't set limits on you tolerating me as your real husband and lover one day. You can take a year, or a decade, or say never if you truly can't get Jascombe's poison out of your system and dream of me instead. I just need to know you will fight for what we two could be together if we both try hard enough.'

'What is it now, Max?' she asked him the question she probably should not.

'Respect to begin with. You must know you are a very beautiful woman and, as I am a healthy adult male, I admit I want you as a man should want his wife, but I am a patient man and will wait and hope that you will eventually want me, too.'

'You should say your wedding vows to a real woman eager to be your wife from the start,' she said.

'Do you really think I could be happy with her, knowing you were stuck at Mynham for the next decade and a half and fighting for your daughters' happiness every hour of the day?' he said as lightly as if they were still easy together as they strolled along this familiar path, although they were nothing of the kind.

They were several correct feet apart and so careful not to touch one another she knew it was a kind lie and he had as many doubts about this marriage as she did.

'And you *are* a real woman, so stop belittling yourself at Jascombe's bidding,' he added as if he found the idea repulsive.

'I want to be one for you, but I'm still not sure I can be,' she said with the almost painful honesty he seemed to have released in her after all those years of pretending. A very small part of her did long to be his eager lover, but the rest wasn't sure she could fight her demons that hard and trust him to make their marriage as wonderful as hers to Edgar had been awful.

'Then we're already halfway there,' he said.

'You are more trusting than I am,' she warned him with one last try to be honest and not put her interests before his.

'I haven't been taught not to trust by the rat that should have adored and valued you ahead of his own twisted and selfish needs, though, have I? You can trust me, I promise you.'

'I know I can,' she replied and shut down any more attempts to save her oldest friend from her need to make sure her children had happy futures. She might, too, if they were very lucky and she was going to marry him anyway and hope it turned out for the best for him as well as for her and her daughters.

'Will you marry me, then, Georgia?' he said. Bless the man, but he even sounded nervous as he gave her the proposal he thought she must want. He took her hand and she felt that stir of something strange deep inside her again and almost snatched it back as if he'd burnt her, but he would be so insulted she simply could not hurt him that deeply.

'Yes, Max, I will,' she answered and saw some strong feeling in his eyes before he bent his head and kissed the back of her hand like a gallant of old.

Now that stir was a sharp heat and promised so much she didn't understand wanting that she flinched. He dropped her hand as if it had scalded him and she was hopeless at whatever their old friendship was turning into.

'If you are sure,' she added after fumbling this so badly.

'I'm sure,' he said so steadily she almost believed him.

'On my wedding day, you told me you were never going to put yourself through all this, Max,' Zach reminded him as they walked to Riverdale Church together so Georgia could be married from her old home this time.

The Duke had offered them Mynham's private chapel when Max had ridden there to tell the man he was going to marry his former daughter-in-law and to request the transfer of guardianship for Georgia's daughters that Ness had promised in that hasty letter. Max still couldn't forgive him for his cruel and rude attempt to reorder Georgia's life and her children's. Or for Ness's original scheme to wed his obnoxious spare son to an innocent in order to make sure his duchy survived.

Why Ness thought Georgia would want a reminder of her disastrous wedding to Jascombe in the same place eight years ago was beyond him and to him it spoke volumes for Ness's insensitivity. Max's fingers threatened to tighten into fists at the very thought of the pompous old fool and they had been doing it a lot lately.

He didn't want to be furious on his wedding day, so he splayed them out and the tug of his fine and gentlemanly gloves reminded him exactly why he was tricked out like the finest dandy in Mayfair on a fine day when he could be busy elsewhere if he wasn't getting married.

He wondered how Georgia was feeling on her second wedding morning. She would not be ecstatic and would not be marrying him at all if Ness hadn't interfered in hers and her daughters' lives, so maybe he had something to thank the old windbag for, although he wasn't quite sure about that yet. Was she nervous, then? Oh, yes, definitely that and he had made her even more so by laying out his conditions for marriage.

He couldn't regret doing it, even so, and he really couldn't make her those solemn promises in the church where they had both been baptised and not mean to honour them. For an awful moment he wondered how he would feel if she turned tail at the last minute and decided she couldn't marry him after all.

The sick feeling in the pit of his stomach said it would be a disaster, but he didn't want to reason his way through the reason why just now. He had to pretend all was well when she had never loved him as passionately as he once loved her and she probably never would.

'I was only twenty at the time and I was trying to distract you,' he told his brother and wished he felt more like the eager, bedazzled bridegroom Zach had been on the day he married Martha when she was already carrying his child.

If Georgia had wed him eight years ago instead of now he could have been a very happy bridegroom two years before his big brother. He could hardly imagine being such a lovelorn youth today and he didn't want to. It was hard enough to live in hope of a true marriage with Georgia's *maybe one day, but definitely not now* promise all the hope they had.

If only their fates had aligned eight years ago he would have been the happiest young man in England and Georgia would not have had to endure Jascombe's brutal tyranny. In the here and now she didn't want to love him and he didn't want to love her, so they were equal this time. It should feel like a firm basis for marriage, but instead it felt as if they were about to build their house on quicksand. He had to cling to a sliver of hope they could make this right one day. It was too late for either of them to back out.

'You sounded very certain about it, but I suppose Georgia Welland was married to another man at the time. I should have realised you didn't want to marry anyone else.'

'You were too much in love to notice anything much on that day and I should have kept my mouth shut. There were plenty more fish in the sea.'

'Funny how you never tried very hard to catch any of them, though, isn't it?'

'I have been busy rescuing the castle you didn't want.'

'And now I know why you threw yourself into restoring Holdfast as if you were desperate for something to distract yourself with.'

'I am a younger son so I needed a purpose in life, but I wasn't distracting myself from my long-lost love, if that's what you think.'

'You do know I would wish you so very happy on your wedding day if you looked as if you were going to be, don't you, Max?'

'Mind your own business, Zach. You wouldn't have welcomed my interference if I had tried to tell you how you felt about Martha on *your* wedding day, so don't try to do it to me on mine.'

'But we are happy,' Zach argued doggedly and

with a concerned brotherly frown, 'we love one another.'

'It's obvious you can't keep your hands off her and even I recognise the signs Martha is increasing again. She was even paler than Georgia last night at that family dinner Mama would insist on throwing for us and I didn't think that was even possible until Martha bolted out of the dining room to cast up her accounts and you raced out after her.'

'Aye, she does suffer for the first two or three months, the poor love. She swears she is delighted to be expecting our next little demon in the New Year, despite the sickness and the prospect of being big with child so soon after the last two.

'She wants our children to grow up together instead of being spaced out like we were for some reason known only to her and, before you ask, I have no idea why she thinks it was a bad idea. I long ago gave up trying to work out Martha's reasoning and usually go along with her nowadays, especially when it suits me so well,' Zach said, looking very smug about his wife's latest project.

Max remembered the marriage of pure convenience his brother had set out to make with one Tolbourne sister and what a contrast that was to the very different sister he had ended up marrying. 'Reason never did have much of a place between you two,' he said.

'True,' Zach said happily.

His brother was so absorbed in thinking about his own marriage he forgot the very different one

Max was about to make as they walked on through Riverdale village together. Max wondered what the harum-scarum boy and girl who once ran wild here would think of the stiffly fashionable people they were today.

'Do you still love her, Max?' Zach asked him abruptly. Why couldn't he have carried on having a contented daydream about his wife instead of asking the question Max was trying so hard not to ask himself?

'Who says that I ever did?' he answered him warily.

'I would have to be daft and short sighted not to know you were fathoms deep in love with Miss Welland before and after she married Jascombe.'

'Maybe, but I was only eighteen and it was calf love.'

'Then why *are* you going to marry her now that you are six and twenty?'

'You ask too many questions,' Max told his brother grumpily.

He wondered why the bride was supposed to be the one who suffered from bridal nerves when his felt stretched nearly to breaking point and he didn't want to be in love with Georgia again. It had hurt too much the first time. And the second, he finally admitted privately as he looked back at the day they had met in that damned wood in the wintry dawn after Jascombe's funeral and he knew he was still in love with her as she sobbed in his arms and told him she could never marry again.

'You are very grumpy on your wedding day. I was ecstatic to be marrying Martha on mine,' Zach said.

'You were so nervous I thought I should have brought smelling salts ready to revive you when you had the vapours.' Max gave a reluctant grin at the memory of his usually cool and composed brother so on fire to wed the love of his life that Max really had wondered if the groom would faint from nerves on his wedding morning.

'You are not acting like I did, Max,' Zach said as if the difference between the fond lover he was that day and the not very hopeful one Max was being today worried him.

Max's reminiscent smile faded as he searched for the right words to lie to his brother that he was so preoccupied with dreams of his wedding night he was silenced by them, but they wouldn't come. 'I'm not, am I?' he admitted at last and shrugged because he couldn't pretend this was the happiest day of his life to his elder brother. It was only the hope of a happy ending for him and Georgia maybe years in the future, if all the faint chances they had worked out the right way and their stars finally aligned.

He wasn't sure if Georgia would ever beat her fear of intimacy and he might be starting a life of bitter frustration rather than the loving and very passionate kind of marriage Zach and Martha enjoyed. Maybe he would need the mistress he didn't want in the end, but it didn't feel right for him to contemplate being unfaithful to his wife before he had even married her, so he wasn't even going to consider it until he knew all hope for them was dead.

'Despite the fact you were such a scrubby brat when we were young and plagued the life out of me, I do still love you, Max. Promise to come to me if you ever need to talk about whatever is troubling you and I promise to listen as if we are both sober adults. And even if you want to weep, come and find me anyway.

'I would be insulted if you shared your misery with anyone else except your wife. I really wish I thought you two were marrying for love and she will be your first and best confidant from now on, but I can't convince myself you are.'

'We are such old and dear friends it's a sort of love,' Max argued feebly.

'Just not the right sort to base a marriage on,' Zach said coolly.

'Not yet,' Max said uncomfortably, very relieved they had finally reached the village church. The vicar was waiting to greet him fondly even after the pranks Master Maxwell Chilton and daredevil Miss Welland played on him in their youth, so it was too late for either of them to have second thoughts.

Chapter Seven

'Ready?' her father asked Georgia and she nodded and smiled as if she really was. She had to be now it came to promising the things Max wanted her to mean one day.

'Ready,' she said as confidently as she could manage with a swarm of butterflies fluttering away in her stomach at the very thought of all those solemn promises.

'At least I can give you away with a light heart this time.'

'What do you mean?'

'I always wondered about Lord Edgar. He was too affable.'

'You hid your doubts very well, then,' she said, surprised they were having this conversation now rather than before her first wedding at Mynham, when it might have done her some good, even if it would have been the scandal of the year if she had jilted Edgar at the altar.

'You and your mother were delighted with the match and Jascombe acted the part of besotted suitor so well I thought I must be imagining things, but I wasn't, was I?'

'No,' she told her father the truth about her first marriage at last. There didn't seem much point pretending she had been deliriously happy with Edgar when he knew she hadn't been and at least today she was marrying a truly good man.

'If you are marrying Max to persuade Ness to give him guardianship of my granddaughters, we can still find another way, Georgia, my love. I don't want you marrying even Max Chilton for all the wrong reasons.'

'I love Max, Papa. It has taken me a stupid amount of time to realise it, but you must admit he is worth loving,' Georgia said, feeling guilty about saying it, but it wasn't exactly a lie.

Max had always been her best friend and it was only an exaggeration to call it love. If she ever did manage to put the past behind her and trust him to stoke this funny little burn only he had ever lit at the heart of her into a blaze, it might even come true one day.

'As you two were as thick as thieves when you were children I shall have to believe you and hope it's the right thing for me to do this time.'

'Please do, Papa, and you know Max will never hurt me,' she said and he nodded and seemed content.

Max wouldn't hurt her, but what if she hurt him?

She walked out to the flower-bedecked barouche on her father's arm and acted the happy bride all the way to the village church even as she struggled with her doubts that this was the right thing for him, although it was her way out of a tense and miserable life at Mynham with her girls.

Her mother was already in church and was no doubt happily anticipating a grandson with a castle to his name one day to add to the two granddaughters of a duke she already prided herself on. Georgia smothered the gloomy thought that her mother would probably be disappointed and so would Max if that was what he wanted from this marriage.

Millie and Helen had gone ahead in her chaise with Leonora and the other bridesmaids and Georgia was glad she had insisted Leonora was one and secretly delighted that Becky had refused to put off her mourning for a day and attend the bride as well. They might have to share a roof after the wedding, but Georgia could ignore that prickly fact today and at least they wouldn't be living in one another's pockets. Becky had her own part of the Castle and could live the independent life she had claimed she wanted and, with any luck, she and Georgia would be able to avoid one another most of the time.

Hope, she reminded herself; it was what today was about. She had to hope she would throw off the past and love Max as he deserved to be loved one day. He would have to hope that she did, too. As her father led her up the aisle she fought tears as Millie and Helen held hands behind her and smiled graciously at their audience. Georgia met Max and his brother at the chancel steps and Leonora passed the girls over to Becky's surprisingly loving care and took Georgia's neat bouquet off her so that she could get married to Max.

He looked so tall and handsome in his wedding finery *she* almost cried, so no wonder both their mothers were pretending not to on either side of the aisle. Max's superfine navy-blue coat emphasised the mature power of his muscular shoulders even if his snowy white linen made him look far too bronzed and healthy to be a Bond Street Beau. Her knees shook as she took in the potent fact of him standing there so smart and solemn and intent on making the sacred oaths they were about to promise one another.

His brother stood at his side with a challenge in his ice-blue eyes cold enough to make her shiver. Max and Zach were so different in looks; Max as dark as their Celtic mother and Zach as fair as their Viking ancestors on his father's side, but their strong features and steely integrity would always give them away as brothers. Zach's wary, warning gaze said mean the vows she was about to make Max or he would never forgive her for her lies.

Apart from the one to obey that she stuttered over, she truly hoped she could mean them all one day. As that one word refused to leave her lips she told herself this was Max and he would never make her do that. She still couldn't push the word past suddenly dry lips and Max's hand tightened on hers for a moment so she looked up at him.

She might never have managed to promise to do that again, even for him, if she hadn't met his eyes properly for the first time today. Wondering at the warm depths of his brown eyes, she forgot Edgar's cruelty and false promises. Yes, it was safe to promise Max what he would never demand of her so she managed to say it when he raised one eyebrow to say she didn't have to mean this one. She had to smile because he understood her so well and today she had to believe the bond they shared would grow even stronger as she made the rest of her vows to him, never mind who else was listening.

At last the vicar triumphantly pronounced them man and wife, and let no man put them asunder, before he told Max he could kiss his bride. She had been so intent on saying her vows and meaning them that she had forgotten that bit. She must have looked startled because Max raised that eyebrow again and his wry look melted the cold knot in her belly at the thought he had a right to do that whenever he wanted to now.

Then he kissed her squarely on her unwarily parted lips and the feel of his firm mouth on hers shocked her to the core. It was such a swift, light kiss she should not have felt much more than his mouth stroking hers and flitting away again. Yet that brief contact made a shiver of something hot and vivid shoot right through her. Her lips pouted of their own accord, as if they wanted more and never mind her shocked mind and tingling body.

But Max had already turned away; he probably only kissed her to make sure he would walk down the aisle with a truly blushing bride on his arm. She clung to the muscular strength of it and waited for her suddenly wobbly legs to stop all this nonsense and do their proper duty again as they walked out into the sunshine together as man and wife.

A sneaky voice deep inside her whispered, *If that's what Maxwell Chilton can do to you without even trying, then how would it feel if he meant it with truly sensual intent in those velvet-brown eyes of his and his magnificent body on fire for you?*

She told it to be quiet and let her concentrate on getting through her second wedding day without anyone suspecting it was less loving than it looked. If she and Max had loved one another, they would be so eager for the wedding night, but she was only eager for the fuss and pretence to be over with so they could get to Holdfast and begin a new life there with her girls. Max would be delighted to be back there as well and maybe they could be content with what they had now and wait for it to grow into something more intimate.

'How many grandpapas and grandmamas have we got now, Mama?' Helen asked Georgia as the newest Chilton family rode back to Riverdale for the wedding feast in the barouche.

'Two of each, just like before,' Millie told her crossly before Georgia could stop being distracted by the memory of Max's swift kiss on her still-hungry mouth and answer her. 'We don't want any more. Remember Duke Grandpapa shouting and Duchess Grandmama saying horrid things about Mama so we ran away?'

Helen looked as if she was about to cry at the reminder of what one set of her grandparents had been like when she stayed with them, but Max intervened before Georgia could reassure her daughters they need never fear such pettish grown-up furies since they were never going near Mynham again if she had anything to do with it.

'I am sure my mother would love to be your extra grandmother if you two ever decide you want one, but she won't insist because she's just not that kind of person,' he said easily.

Millie looked very serious as she thought about the idea, then nodded as if she was ready to accept his word they could take their time deciding whether it was a good idea or not. Georgia was so glad her girls already trusted Max and knew they would never have a reason not to, so she left him to get on with being their new stepfather.

'We already like Aunty Becky and her baby, don't forget,' Helen told her big sister earnestly and looked a lot more cheerful now she had been subtly reminded the Dowager Lady Elderwood was not at all like the Duchess of Ness.

'I like my sister and the baby, too, although little Phoebe can be very noisy at times, I'm afraid,' Max said after a pause so Georgia could step in if she wanted to, but she gave him a wry smile, then let her thoughts drift as he carried on the good work.

What if the last eight years had never happened? her inner idiot speculated. *What if she was riding back to her childhood home next to her new husband after years of stubbornly refusing to admit that he was the love of her life and now she had finally given in and agreed to marry him after all? What if they were about to have a wedding night unsullied by her memories of the first one? Would they sit much closer and spare a rueful smile for his long campaign to make her see sense and her ridiculous refusal to do so until now?*

That Georgia would have no idea how suffocating it felt to live inside a marriage with a man who did not respect her and only cared about his twisted needs and desires and getting her with child until she produced a boy. How *would* it feel to have been courted for so long she gave in at last because she was weak with longing for the mature and potent man at her side?

She danced her fantasy Max and Georgia up Hold-fast Castle's vast state staircase and into the master of the castle's lofty bedchamber and had to snap out of her daydream before she said something stupid to the real one, or flinched away from the whole idea, despite that stupid tingle of awareness of him as a man that had started up again with a vengeance thanks to his kiss at the altar.

She sat up straight and shot Max a wary glance, hoping he had missed her softened expression and dreamy eyes. It was impossible to wish her marriage to Edgar undone because it had given her Millie and Helen and this wasn't a fantasy, it was real life. Max seemed as coolly controlled as ever so she stopped making up stories in her head of how things could have been if she had had the sense not to marry Edgar eight years ago. She had been that silly and they both had to live with whatever they could salvage from their old friendship and hope they could forge a more loving one in future.

'Mama! Look at all those people waving at us,' Millie shouted and Georgia felt tears threatening yet again and decided she was turning into a watering pot.

There were so many people lining the road up to her father's house, waiting to cheer and wave at two long-ago partners in mischief who had married one another, that it touched her deeply. She smiled and waved back and hoped this looked like the happiest day of her life so far. It should be and maybe years from now she would look back on it and reimagine herself as a loving and beloved bride who had just married the man of her dreams. She felt a shiver of that oddly hot and almost hopeful feeling slide through her once again and puzzling over it, and this very different wedding day, made her move through the rest of it in a daze.

At last it was time for them all to go back to Holdfast and she joined Max and the girls in the first carriage of the procession with Leonora and Huggins riding in the next one. Becky was going to stay with her mother for a week before she returned and Georgia suspected she was wishing she had agreed to live at Flaxonby Dower House now she would have to share Holdfast with her new sister-in-law.

Yet who would have thought this would happen when Georgia set out to visit her parents and Aunt Isobel? Not her, she decided as the grim old fortress loomed on the horizon and she was tempted to shiver at the sight of its most forbidding watch towers and defensive walls.

She didn't because Max loved the place and would be hurt if he saw it and even to her it felt like a place of safety. That might be because Max owned it and she was safe with him and so were her daughters. Yet its forbidding exterior hid a softer, friendlier face as the rambling old place had turned in on itself to protect its occupants in wilder days when these borders were fought over by English barons and Scottish lairds.

'Welcome home, Mrs Chilton,' Max said softly, after he jumped down first so he could hand her out of the carriage.

'Why, thank you, Mr Chilton,' she said lightly.

She had learned self-control in such a hard school he would have no idea that the feel of his long, work-roughened fingers wrapped around hers had sent another hot shiver shooting through her until she felt oddly warm all the way down to her toes and wanted to draw them away, but didn't.

'And welcome to Holdfast Castle, Miss Amelia and Miss Helen,' he said with a bow to the young ladies who stepped out of the carriage with his help, looking so quaintly regal Georgia had to bite her lip to fight the chuckle they would find insulting.

'Can we be Miss Chilton as well as Mama being Mrs Chilton now you are married to her, Max?' Millie asked as she stepped down from the carriage like a young lady for once instead of an urchin in a tearing hurry.

'I will ask the lawyers what they can do,' he said rather hoarsely. Georgia could see how moved he was by her girls' ready acceptance of him.

They had never really had a father and she knew she had done the right thing for them, even if she still had doubts about what she had done to Max. She could not mean all of the solemn oaths they had exchanged yet and that felt so wrong on their wedding night. He deserved so much better from his wife and it felt shocking to realise that was who she was now—Mrs Maxwell Chilton.

She was so glad to shed Edgar's name and title that she ran up the stairs after her girls as they explored their new home with a light heart. She even began to share Max's delight in the place as he showed them around the nurseries and family rooms and it felt so safe she might love it, too, one day.

Millie and Helen settled into life at Holdfast as if this was their best adventure yet. Georgia hoped they felt the same in the winter when wind whistled down stone corridors and through the still untouched rooms. They would probably still love it and it was the perfect playground for two enterprising little girls. There were too many places for them to hide in for her peace of mind and she was determined to learn the Castle inside and out so she could find them when they escaped their lessons or their beds.

It was time to make sure her supposed little angels were in bed as Leonora would have handed them over to Nanny by now. Georgia went up to the nursery Max had made out of a suite of rooms in the Tudor wing of the main house because he said children should not have to live on dusty old top floors or neglected corners nobody else wanted. That was one more dream he must have had before she came along and spoiled it for him.

She hesitated on the stairs, feeling guilty about him getting these nurseries ready for children of his own one day that he would probably never have. She must live with what she had done to him and make herself carry on. She stopped abruptly outside the door when she heard Max's deep voice inside and realised he was reading her girls a bedtime story and they obviously weren't missing her.

Hearing what he was saying, she nearly interrupted because she usually skipped past that particular story for fear of frightening Helen and giving them nightmares, but Max was telling his own version. Two girls very like them stole the Giant's clothes and put pepper in his porridge and it made him cry so hard he was put to bed by his nanny instead of chasing after them with a cleaver when they escaped with his gold.

'And if anyone with similar names and the same idea tries to pull tricks like that here, I will chop their beanstalk down to make sure they cannot leave *my* castle, so don't even think about it, you two,' she heard him say. He was making sure her little demons didn't get any more ideas for mischief than they already had, wasn't he?

'But we don't want to escape from this one,' Helen protested and Georgia knew her thumb was in her mouth because only a mother's ears could hear past it from out here.

'We want to stay here for ever,' Millie said and she knew her eldest daughter was trying to sound wide awake as usual. She would fight sleep until she couldn't keep her eyes open any longer and Georgia smiled at the sound of her elder daughter protesting she wasn't in the least bit tired.

They were so absorbed Georgia risked looking through the partly open door and saw Max had perched on the side of Helen's bed so she could snuggle into his shoulder. He was ever so gently sliding away from her so he could tuck her in. She knew Millie would be sitting up in her bed, pretending not to be sleepy at all.

'You can stay here as long as you like,' Max said softly.

How did he know to make his voice softer and softer as their eyelids drooped over sleepy eyes despite their resolution to stay awake all night? His elder sister Joan had six children and Zachary and Martha were racing to catch her up and Georgia knew Max would be an interested and engaged uncle. Of course he knew more about children than most gentlemen his age would bother to learn about their funny little ways.

'Kiss,' Helen demanded sleepily and Georgia shifted to see Max's face.

He didn't look horrified, he looked amused and tender and maybe a little bit wistful, or was she imagining that last bit? A guilty conscience was a terrible thing and she could be putting a deep longing for a child of his own in Max's thoughtful gaze when it probably wasn't what he was thinking at all. He kissed Helen and her well-worn peg doll when she insisted it needed one, too.

'Goodnight, Max,' Millie said quite loudly. Georgia saw him put a finger to his lips and point towards the other bed, so Helen must have dropped straight to sleep already.

'Goodnight, Minx,' he replied softly and bent to kiss her forehead.

But Millie threw her arms around his neck and whispered very loudly, 'I love you, Max.'

'I love you, too, Miss Millie-Amelia,' he said gruffly, and Georgia suspected he was fighting tears as well as her.

He didn't know what a huge difference he was making to the girls' lives already, so he didn't have the same excuse as she did. She scrubbed her tears away and almost crept off so he didn't know she had ever been there, but she had been a coward for too long, so she stayed.

He left the night nursery after a soft goodnight to Nanny and it was Georgia's turn to put a finger to her lips when he started at the sight of her and she was the one who had to lean over and softly close the door behind him. Her heartbeat raced so wildly as she felt the warmth of his body that those nerves of hers got excited again although they hadn't even touched one another. Max looked as if he was about to say something and she beckoned him to follow her down the stairs until they were out of earshot.

'Thank you, Max, you have made them feel safe again and you have no idea what a blessing it is to them and to me.'

'I told them stories because they were overtired and Nanny was at her wits' end to know what to do with them,' he said as if he needed an excuse for doing what he had just done. 'I don't want to usurp your role,' he added stiffly.

'Don't be ridiculous, I love the fact they trust you. I never want them to hesitate and be afraid to show their feelings as they were when we got them back from my former father-in-law, so timid and unlike themselves I knew I had been right to worry about them under his roof. You are so natural with them. Why would I even want to deprive them of the kind of father they have always longed for and never had?'

He turned his head away as if he didn't want her to see how he felt about the idea he was one of those to her beloved daughters now and she knew he was hiding too much emotion and not too little. 'They are fine girls, even if they do have enough energy for a cartload of monkeys.'

'They are and they have and thank you, but they are your girls as well now, if you don't mind having a readymade family thrust upon you.'

'No,' he said and there was the husky tone in his voice again to tell her he was struggling with emotions he was unwilling to let her know about. 'They are a credit to me and I haven't even had to try,' he added to make a joke out of her thanks when she wanted him to be serious and talk to her about a subject she had thought was neutral enough not to snarl up their tongues like this.

'Please feel free to share that part of bringing them up as well, but you have made them feel secure in their own skins again, Max, and please don't dismiss that as if it's not very important. They haven't had a single nightmare since we came here and you don't know what a relief that is for all of us.'

'I can guess,' he said grimly and at least they had their fury at what the Duke and Duchess had done to Millie and Helen in a few short weeks in common.

'I will see you at dinner, then,' she said as they ran out of it and she couldn't think of anything else to say, but did risk an encouraging smile.

'I forgot to tell you I am engaged tonight,' he said abruptly, as if she had bitten him instead of smiled and he had marched away before she could even argue that was the first she had heard of it.

Of course he wasn't engaged. He would not have been upstairs inventing bedtime stories for her girls and telling her it was nothing if he was due to be somewhere else very soon. She stared at the door he had disappeared through and tried to remember where it led, but she knew he was only using it as a way to avoid her so it didn't matter.

Tears welled up for her own sake this time and she mourned the ease and freedom to say whatever came into their heads the young Max and Georgia had once enjoyed. She missed their friendship and not his touch or the complex thoughts in his grown-up, yet so dearly familiar dark eyes. She didn't want more of his light-as-air kisses or to feel his firm lips on hers and especially not anything more serious to smother her with masculine urgency and make it feel as if he was choking her as she tried to shut all feeling down and endure…

No, stop that right now, Georgia Chilton!

It simply would not do and it would never be like that between her and Max. She was defiling what they could have with what Edgar was. His poison had done too much damage already and she wanted to cut him out of her thoughts and emotions. Most of all she wanted to be able to tell Max what she wanted, to have the luxury of his company while she worked her way past her jagged old fears of intimacy even with him.

How was she ever going to manage it without him close by to help and encourage her? But apparently he couldn't even stay here and talk to her. Hurt closed her in on herself again as she stood still for a long moment and tried to gather the courage to meet Leonora's eyes over the nearly empty dinner table and tell her about Max's fictional engagement elsewhere.

He was clumsy and a fool; Max paused in midstride and looked back at his castle in the twilight. He wanted to go back so much he stumbled and righted himself before turning away again and heading anywhere else but there. He could hear a distant farm dog barking and wondered if its senses were so acute it could hear or even smell him out here in the near darkness where he didn't belong. It was wrong and ridiculous of him, but he couldn't go back home yet.

Sharing the same castle with his wife when she

smiled at him and made him feel like that clumsy and tongue-tied boy again felt impossible. He had been so desperate to lean forward just a step or so and kiss her temptingly parted lips until he remembered she would freeze or gag and back away, so terrified of him and his urgent desire for her as a real wife he had to walk away.

It was that or risk everything they would have to build so slowly it felt like agony to even think of right now. He wanted her so much, longed for her to be receptive and responsive as he knew she could be if only Jascombe hadn't spoiled the act of love for her by forcing the exact opposite of love on her like the brute he was.

It was hardly a week since the wedding and Max felt as if he was being torn apart by wants and needs he didn't even want to think about as he walked on more carefully as night fell all around him, yet somehow he couldn't help himself. Even the certainty no other woman but Georgia would do for him felt like an added torture tonight. With the thought of all the months, if not years, of this endless and frustrated desire for his own wife goading him on he even wondered if he might do better to walk on and on and not go back.

Coward, the stir of a breeze whispered as he fumbled along in the near dark.

His feet were taking him somewhere without much thought, but he realised he was heading for the only woodland his greedy predecessor as owner of Holdfast had left standing. Alderman Tolbourne would not have done so if he had known about it, of course, but somehow it remained a secret from both him and the woodsmen he had brought in to fell every stand of timber on the estate large enough to sell.

Either the people on the estate didn't know about an ancient woodland in a remote valley up on the Holdfast Moors, which seemed highly unlikely, or they had decided not to tell their rapacious landlord about it.

He loved the place either way and was so glad it had survived to remind him of the mossy old woods on the Flaxonby Estate where he and Georgia had enjoyed some of their best adventures as children. He groaned out loud as he realised how entangled their lives were and remembered how easy they had been together before he fell in love with her and she didn't fall in love with him. Maybe she never would now.

That idea felt so desolate that even his mighty frustration died down a little and he could stride on more freely as a sliver of moon rose and his eyes adjusted to the darkness. Because he was so frustrated, he knew he wasn't to be trusted in her company. That old lovely uncomplicated ease between them was never going to return unless she learned to tolerate him as a husband, of course, and that idea didn't even bear thinking about right now.

Reaching what felt like sanctuary, he breathed in the mossy, leafy scent of woodland that felt as old as time itself. He tried to fade into it as if he was more part of nature than the legal owner of it even if there was something about it that felt as if it couldn't be owned by man.

He heard little flutters and flusters in the undergrowth to say he shouldn't be here, but he ignored them and sat on a summer-dry boulder by the stream at the heart of it and tried to gather enough willpower and serenity to go back home. He needed to sleep just enough to be ready for another day, pretending to be civilised and energetic Maxwell Chilton when he didn't feel like being either of those things any more.

Georgia told herself knowing his ancient fortress and its later additions better might help her see why Max loved it so much. She paused at a large window high in the old keep one of the later DeMayne lords must have installed when the threat of attack faded. The view was breathtaking—no wonder Max's ancestors had chosen to build their castle here. Without the sheltering trees later generations had planted to break the worst of the wind, its lofty position gave a distant view of the road between England and Scotland. When those countries were still fighting over this land it must have been a great advantage to see trouble coming before it got here.

Georgia shuddered at the idea of such troubled times and thanked heaven this was now, so Max didn't have to fight at the whim of a king and she didn't have to stand here worrying about him or their home and family.

Not that they were likely to have one of those when she was still afraid of intimacy and he was avoiding her. He was always home in time for the girls' supper and playtime and they demanded a story from him before they would sleep now and he was so kind and patient with them she managed not to mind if they didn't need her to do it instead. Yet once they were asleep he would dine with her and Leonora, wish them a civil goodnight and that would be the last his wife saw of him until whatever time he couldn't avoid her the next day.

She was so restless she had gone on learning his castle by candlelight or moonlight, not because she would hear Max hammering at a floorboard or mending an old door and feel a sort of connection with him. Even from a distance she could hear it was hard work and his stubborn labour on the unrestored parts of the castle after a hard day on the estate was meant to exclude her from his life.

He *had* reluctantly agreed, in principle, to use her money to carry out repairs he couldn't keep up with on his own, but he hadn't spent any of it yet. She knew he was using work on the castle as a wall between them. He had made sure all but the most impersonal contact was kept to a minimum between them and she supposed she should be grateful for such stern consideration. She still feared taking him to her bed when she was awake, but she was having such ridiculous dreams about him now and he was doing nothing to teach her to be less timid.

She was a wife, but not a real one, and that was what she had wanted when she came here to beg him to marry her just a few weeks ago. Getting her own way had never felt less satisfying than it did now and Max was the one who had argued for a proper marriage. Didn't that mean they should be spending a lot more time together so she could learn how to know and trust him as an adult as well as the boy she once knew so well?

Whatever it meant, it felt ridiculous of her to stand here yearning for something she would shy away from if Max was watching her with the deep sensual need she knew he was capable of in his warm brown eyes. She stretched and felt the tiredness of not having enough sleep in her limbs, so goodness knew what his felt like. The nights here felt endless and it wasn't because she was afraid Max would come to her bed before she was ready for him. She just didn't want to toss and turn in her lonely bed, or repeat the silly dreams she had been having about him now they were actually married and he didn't seem to want her to share his.

The intimacy marriage should mean must have loosed an inner wanton she never even knew was hiding inside her, waiting to want such impossible things. She shivered with whatever this was she felt about Max as her lover when she was awake. Asleep she had the most outrageous fantasies of Max intent on loving her and so heartbreakingly handsome in her bed, with every ounce of his sensual attention focused on her as she welcomed him with open arms.

She still didn't want to do anything about them when she was awake and shivered again at the thought of those dreams up here at her favourite window in broad daylight. Best to forget the mornings when she woke up in a tangle of bedclothes with his name on her lips and knew Max was already up and long gone.

She knew he would not knock on the door between their bedchambers. He had locked it the first day they got here as man and wife and handed her the key. She wasn't even going to think about those shocking dreams of him, all lover like and rampant for her again. Instead she would go and occupy herself with the housekeeping she had begun to get under control.

Such things were low down on Max's list of priorities while he was busy getting the place habitable and repairing damage all over the ruthlessly exploited and demoralised Holdfast Estate. They would have to entertain his neighbours now Max was married and she didn't want them speculating about the state of their marriage if she didn't take up her role as the most important lady in the district soon, so there was plenty for her to do here, in the daytime.

She sighed at her stupid yearning for her husband's company and stared unseeingly at the starkly beautiful land below and told herself the heat was making the landscape look as if it was shimmering and she wasn't going to cry. She was about to turn away from the window when movements in the distance caught her eye and she saw a travelling chaise beginning the long climb up the hill.

Becky must be coming home, so the honeymoon was officially over. Not that she and Max had had one, but Becky didn't know that. She sighed again and got ready to face her sister-in-law's unspoken hostility and tried to look on the bright side—maybe Max would spend more time with his family now his little sister was home.

Chapter Eight

In some ways, Becky's return felt like a good thing since Max joined them for breakfast now and again, if he knew Becky would be there. In others, Georgia felt even more unwanted and awkward with two Chiltons avoiding her. Apparently Becky's little daughter found it impossible to settle in the evening unless her mother was there to soothe her to sleep and comfort her if she woke up, or so she said.

Leonora was trying not to become the buffer between Georgia and her sister-in-law when Becky decided it would be rude not to dine with her brother's wife one more time. She began to wish Becky had gone somewhere else and, although it might make a public rift between them, at least then Georgia wouldn't have to tiptoe around her new home feeling like an unwelcome guest.

She let matters drift for a while, but finally decided she had nothing to lose by confronting Becky. Catching her alone at the breakfast table one morning after Max had left on whatever business he planned to exhaust himself with that day, Georgia invited Becky into her private sitting room to explain why she was behaving as if Georgia carried a contagious disease. Becky looked so shocked by a direct challenge that she meekly followed her in and seemed to be searching for a bland excuse.

'I know we have never been close,' Georgia told her as soon as the door was safely closed behind them, 'but we have to live under the same roof until it is less obvious you are leaving Holdfast because you hate me.'

'It's not that,' Becky finally managed to say, but as she avoided Georgia's gaze her denial didn't sound very convincing.

'What is it then? My girls are old enough now to notice you avoid me like the plague and I might not do it for myself, but I will always fight for their peace of mind.'

'I don't hate you. I just can't stand watching you break Max's heart all over again,' Becky burst out as if she had been trying not to say it ever since she had heard he was going to marry Georgia in such haste that she had no chance to argue him out of it.

'Why would I even want to be so cruel?' Georgia asked blankly.

'I don't know—why were you last time?'

'Who says I was?' she countered and tried to gather enough sense to fight back. 'And why would he confide in you instead of me, *if* what you say is true and I doubt it.'

'Of course he didn't confide in me, he's a man, isn't he? I knew you were his private obsession, though, and it was your marriage to Lord Edgar that drove him so far into himself I used to worry he would never truly come back. It took him owning this place and the hard work of getting it repaired and the estate back in profit to teach him to value himself as he should.

'If you make him feel worthless again, he has nowhere to go now that you two are married. If you reject him now, how do you expect him to pick himself up and carry on with his life, Georgia? You are inside his castle now instead of in London so he can't learn to forget you here, can he?'

'If he didn't confide in you, how do you know?' Georgia argued numbly and had to cling to the idea Becky must be wrong.

'I watched him make a cake of himself over you so often before you went off to London that I thought you must know how he felt and you had either ignored his feelings or turned him down. I admit I did hate you then, especially after his first year at Cambridge.

'He came home for the summer so unlike himself we were all worried he would work himself into a brain fever. I sneaked into his bedroom to see why he was struggling so hard to translate some musty old classical text that usually came so easily to him that he barely had to think about it. I went through the notes on his desk to see why it was such hard work.'

'What *was* it about, then?' Georgia asked impatiently since his thoughts on a seven-year-old Greek or Latin puzzle didn't seem very important right now.

'You,' Becky said starkly.

'You mean he wrote something personal and left it lying about where anyone could read it?' she challenged. Becky blushed and looked guilty.

'Of course not, but he had spent so long scratching away at his papers in his room I picked the lock to see what he was writing so frantically when I peeped through the keyhole.'

Becky's cool blue eyes went even cooler as she remembered how Max had shut himself away from the family he loved so much and made his little sister so anxious she had played peeping Tom.

'Zach managed to persuade him to go out for a ride. I took the key from a room I knew would unlock Max's door if I jiggled it the right way so I could see if there was anything we could do to help him.'

'What was it, then?' Georgia said.

'A few words written over and over again as if his life depended on him learning them by heart. *I will forget her...she's married... I must forget her... I can forget her...why can't I forget her?* He had written it time after time in a great pile, with more pages torn up on the floor, and don't you dare say it was about anyone else but you, because that will make me so angry.'

'Why didn't he tell me, then?'

Tears came perilously close when she thought of how miserable she and Max had both been in their separate spaces that summer. She had been recovering from the birth of her first child—loving her little girl, from the tips of Millie's sparse baby curls to her tiny, perfect toes, and hating her baby's father all the time she did so.

She dreaded returning to the marriage bed so Edgar could father a son next time and all that time Max was miserably in love with her, Lord Edgar Jascombe's terrified wife. She had a hard time believing Max was deeply in love with her all those years ago, but Becky was right. Who else was there?

'You must have known that he loved you,' Becky accused her, 'and I'm not sure you love him even now.'

'I didn't know, Becky, truly,' she said, but she could see that Becky didn't believe her.

'You two ran wild together for so long—of course he fell in love with you as soon as he thought he was old enough to love you as a man,' she said scornfully. 'Even I knew he only had eyes for you and I was fifteen. You were three years older and happy to whistle him down the wind as if he had no real feelings and he had so many more for you than you ever deserved. I could have slapped you.'

'Friendship isn't love.'

'It must have grown out of it for him, even if it didn't for you.'

'Maybe it did, but I can't—no, I won't discuss my relationship with my husband with anyone but him. I am his wife and I owe him my loyalty.'

'Just not your love,' Becky said flatly. 'Well, I can't simply stand by and watch you break his heart all over again. Don't you dare shake your head at me as if you wouldn't dream of hurting him, because I know how much you did so eight years ago. He wasn't himself when he came back from your husband's funeral, either.

'Heaven knows what you said or did to him then, because he drove himself as if twenty demons were on his shoulders when he came back to Holdfast after watching you mourn a man who wasn't even fit to black Max's boots.'

'You have no idea what you're talking about,' Georgia lied uneasily. 'I only spoke to him alone for a few minutes at the time.'

'Goodness knows how you managed even that much when you were supposed to be an inconsolable widow.'

Georgia couldn't meet Becky's eyes as she thought about why she had looked to Max for consolation on a bleak winter morning and felt ashamed of herself for asking for it now she knew he had loved her as a boy. Maybe he still did when he held and comforted her and she had no idea her dearest friend had ever wanted to be more than that to her.

'I wasn't,' she said as if the words had escaped of their own accord.

'You weren't what?'

'Inconsolable.'

Silence as Becky wrinkled her nose with revulsion, then seemed to think again and looked puzzled and then horrified. 'Oh, my heavens—that's it, isn't it?' she said as if she had been struck by a truly shocking notion.

'That's what?' Georgia bluffed uneasily.

'Your precious Lord Edgar treated you badly, didn't he? That explains why Max was so furious and hurt and driven when he got back from your husband's funeral.'

Georgia was too horrified by everything she had just learned to pretend Becky was imagining things.

'Your first husband was a beast, wasn't he?' Becky prompted relentlessly.

'Yes,' she finally whispered and met Becky's gaze as bravely as she could.

'I'm so sorry, Georgia,' Becky whispered back as if she had opened Pandora's Box by accident and all the miseries of the world had poured out as she tried to slam the lid back down again.

Georgia winced to recall Max saying the same words to her five years ago when she told him what Edgar had done. 'I have no idea why you are apologising to me,' she said.

'Because you were very nearly right—I have come very close to hating you. I still think you were an idiot to ignore Max and marry a noble brute, but now I pity you as well.'

'I don't want your pity,' Georgia challenged her with a glare. 'Pity makes me less, it makes me pitiable and I refuse to be so ever again.'

'It strikes me you refused it when you were wed to a sly beast,' Becky said with a wry smile that respected Georgia's courage, if not her brains for marrying Edgar in the first place.

'I couldn't let my girls grow up hearing their father being called a brute and me his victim.'

'Thank God my Jack was a true gentleman in every sense of the word, but I would do the same for Phoebe.'

'But you married a hero and I married a beast.'

'My hero is still dead,' Becky said bleakly and Georgia could see the appalling grief behind her quiet declaration and wished she could hug her, but she was too afraid of being shrugged off and knew it was probably the last thing Becky wanted.

'True—can I pity you and your daughter for such a tragic loss?'

'Just this once if you really must, but only so I can pity you back once, too.'

'I am so sorry your Captain Jack died a hero, then, Becky.'

'I'm sorry Lord Edgar was a villain and not in the least bit sorry *he's* dead.'

'We are almost equal, then.'

'I'm more sorry than you are. I should have known there was more to Max's refusal to talk about you than I thought when he set about mending his precious castle as if it had to be done in double quick time five years ago.'

'You must have been busy falling in love at the time so why would you think about me and my woes?'

'I really didn't like you at the time.'

'You don't like me much now.'

'I could learn.'

'If I make Max happy?'

'Yes, but now I shall expect him to make you happy as well.'

'That's progress,' Georgia replied with the glimmer of a smile.

'And I like your daughters; you have made a good job of raising them so far.'

'Was that a compliment?'

Becky shrugged.

'I am almost overwhelmed,' Georgia said. Who would have thought her prickly sister-in-law would approve of something she had done?

'Don't get used to it,' Becky told her half seriously. 'Until you make my brother truly happy you had better be thankful they filled in the moat last century.'

'I will stay away from the battlements as well.'

'Do,' Becky said with a severe nod and they were both silent while they rearranged their opinions, or at least Georgia hoped so.

'How does it feel to love a man to the edge of reason, Becky?' she heard herself ask impulsively, but she really wanted to know.

'It feels…' Becky hesitated and her eyes went

dreamy and then looked so hurt and sad Georgia wished she hadn't asked.

'That was clumsy. I'm sorry; I should not have asked such a personal question.'

'No, don't make me into a sad little widow. I loved Jack too much to be less than he would want me to be. It feels wondrous; I can't find the right words to explain. It's just so warm and close and delicious you feel as if you will never truly be apart again.'

'You have explained it very well and you loved your Jack very much, didn't you?'

'I loved him enough to try to forget he was a soldier every day he was one, even when we were on the march and we could only snatch closeness in small packages. I loved him enough not to persuade him to sell out because he thought it was his duty to fight for his country, but I feared for him every day and I was quite right.'

'He was brave, but maybe you were braver,' Georgia said and Becky cried and she even allowed Georgia to hold her as she wept.

After Becky's heartwrenching tale of Max ordering himself not to love her over and over again when she was already married to Edgar, she had a job not to cry, too. Then Becky scrubbed at her cheeks with her handkerchief as if she was furious at her own weakness and why was it considered one when she had such good reason to cry?

'Love is always worth it, Georgia,' she said earnestly. 'I shall never regret loving Jack with all my heart even now he's gone and I miss him so much.'

Georgia yearned to feel such wholehearted, unguarded love for Max. She almost felt it stirring and shifting deep in her heart, but she wasn't a wholehearted and unguarded person any more. Yet he was right. All the time she was guarding herself from feeling anything much Edgar had still won. If Becky was right, love was worth taking risks for and it was time she stopped being such a coward.

Chapter Nine

'Why did you marry me, Max?'

'What?' he yelped as if Georgia had stung him. The question came at him out of the night and he should never have allowed her to creep up on him while he was holding a hammer. He dropped it hastily and added a limp sounding, 'Why?' while he tried to think of an answer that would make her go away again, before he begged her to take him into her bed and never mind why.

'I need to know,' she said and he didn't want to tell her.

He had wondered the same thing so many times lately, despite the joy of seeing her children blossom and having a family around him just as he dreamt he might before Georgia burst back into his life and turned it upside down again.

'I needed a wife and couldn't endure the thought of Ness and his Duchess playing tug-o'-war with your daughters and you having to watch them,' he managed to say and felt quite proud of himself.

'And?' she demanded as he felt frustrated and a little bit angry with her for not taking his reasons for marrying her as final and going away.

'And I thought we had discussed this as much as it needs discussing when we agreed to marry one another in Zach's park that morning.'

'Becky says you were in love with me when we were young,' she said bluntly and he barely suppressed a groan.

'My little sister should learn to keep her mouth shut,' he grumbled and could not look at Georgia in case he saw pity in her lovely eyes.

'No, she should not and don't you dare tell her so because I'm glad she told me.'

'Glad I suffered as only a very young and inarticulate youth can from calf love?' he said as if it was almost a joke. It really wasn't, so he glared at a plank of green oak and wished she would go before he broke down and begged her to love him now, or at least tolerate him in her bed if he wooed her carefully enough.

'I wish I had known,' she said as if she was almost as uncomfortable with this subject as he was. Why was she persisting with it, then?

'Would it have made any difference?'

'Yes, of course it would. I would have refused Edgar for one thing. You were my best friend and knowing you loved me would have made it wrong for me to marry him.'

'You wouldn't have married me, though. Not a boy of eighteen without a title and a grand house or many prospects; your mother would never have let you.'

'Papa would if he thought we loved one another enough, although I expect he would have made us wait a year or two.'

'Ah, but first you would have had to love me back—as a man and not a gawky boy—and you didn't, did you?'

'I don't know, Max,' she said sadly. 'I was so young and silly and full of my own importance and Mama's warped ideas I don't think I knew what love was.'

'Maybe I didn't, either,' he said, defending himself because he really had loved her then and when he was one and twenty and it was even more hopeless than when she was married to another man. He was trying so hard not to love her again and sometimes he thought the effort of keeping it at bay was going to drive him to drink. 'And I did try to tell you once, but you were not listening.'

'You did?' she said, looking shocked and puzzled. So much for his grand declaration all those years ago when she couldn't even remember the day a stammering boy was stopped in mid-fluster by the entrance of smooth and sophisticated Lord Edgar Jascombe.

She had been so puzzled by what he was trying, and failing, to say at the time that she had looked relieved at the interruption. Jascombe must have seen and heard more than she did since Max suffered that beating the next night. He supposed it took Jascombe a day to find bullies skilled and discreet enough to only half kill him and make sure he was out of the way while Jascombe stole his love. No doubt doing it had added spice to the whole sorry business for the devious little rat.

'The day before I was injured I tried to tell you how much I adored you, but I couldn't get the words out and you seemed to think it was a joke. Then I heard about your marriage while I was at home recovering and there was no point in trying to say it again.'

'Now I remember! I thought you meant you loved me like a brother, as we had been such good friends, and that was why you insisted on being in London when I was there. I assumed you were there to make sure I chose the right husband. I even felt annoyed with you when you glowered at my suitors because I thought you were being overprotective.'

'No, I meant every glower and grumble, young idiot that I was.'

'You were not,' she defended the boy against the mature man. 'I secretly thought it was wonderful you wanted to look out for me since you knew Mama was so in love with the idea of a title she wouldn't fight off improper advances from anyone who had one.'

'Some protector I was when you married Jascombe anyway.'

'I can't tell you how much I wish you had managed to tell me you loved me that day. My life would have been so different if only you had and I must have hurt you so badly.'

'I mended in more ways than one after I was set upon and sent home and you still wouldn't have had me as a scrubby youth if I had managed to say I loved you. Jascombe could dazzle and outdo me and he was a grown man. You thought me such a boy you didn't seem to want to listen to what I was trying to say to you that day and I wasn't very good at saying it,' he told her with a shrug and a wry smile he hoped said *Ah, well, it was a long time ago.*

'I would have thought harder about his dazzling and outdoing if you had stayed and tried again. I would have said no to you as well, but I wouldn't have married him either.'

'It's all water under the bridge. You did marry him and I grew up. We are both very different people now.'

'And you married me for old times' sake?'

'I married you because you needed a husband and I will need a wife one day if you can bear to be one to me. We have had the rest of this conversation already and it isn't the right time or place to rehash it.'

'When will it be, then?'

'I don't know—maybe when you make up your mind whether you can tolerate me as a husband or not,' he said rashly and saw her flinch and felt ashamed of himself. 'Please forget I said that,' he added wearily and turned to pick up his hammer and hoped she would take the hint and leave him to his frustrated solitude.

'I want to, but I'm too afraid,' she said bravely and he didn't want bravery from his wife, he wanted the impossible. He wanted her to love him and he didn't want to love her again unless she did—stalemate, then—checkmate even.

'You humble me, Georgia, but I still wish you would go away.'

'Very well,' she said and he had to be glad because he was only human and the impossible was still impossible.

Max wasn't sure if he was relieved or sad when Becky's revelation didn't change much between him and Georgia. If anything, they were more wary with each other than they had been before. She seemed more worried about hurting him than she was about trusting him with her most vulnerable inner self and she would have to do that if they were ever going to make love. He didn't want her to tiptoe around him because he had once loved her and she wasn't too sure that he didn't still love her now. But that was what she was doing now.

He let out a sigh as softly as he could manage. Being married to Georgia was remarkably easy in some ways, but in others it was a refined form of torture. From the moment they had walked back down the aisle together as man and wife, he had been racked with frustration and something even more painful that he didn't want to think about too deeply. He had promised her patience and it felt all the more crucial for him to keep his promises because Jascombe had lied through his teeth. That didn't mean it was easy, but here they still were and hope wasn't dead yet.

'It was an interesting evening,' he lied as the carriage rumbled on through the moonlit fields.

'Yes,' she said, as if she had been deep in thought and he wished they were of him. 'Miss Stevens plays very well, don't you think?' she added.

Who the devil was Miss Stevens? Ah, yes, the musical one. 'Better than the usual run of accomplished young ladies, I suppose,' he replied carefully. He hadn't spared Miss Stevens or her playing much attention while he was busy with trying not to stare at his own wife all evening like a mooncalf.

'Hmm, and she is quite the beauty with it.'

'I suppose she is pretty enough.'

'You should know since you watched her so intently while she played that Mozart sonata you should be able to list her perfections without a pause.'

'I did?'

'Yes, you did,'

'I was wool-gathering.'

'Yet she would have suited you very well if I had not got in the way, wouldn't she, Max?'

'I can't say I have ever noticed her in that way either before or after we were married, but she is a fine pianist and Caisters is clearly enamoured with her, so perhaps they will be able to play duets whenever they choose to before the year is out.'

'Clever,' she said flatly and he wondered if he should keep his mouth shut and give the occasional hmm of agreement or *tell me more* some husbands seemed to have perfected.

'Not really, I meant musical duets,' he said with a grimace at the shadowy landscape they were passing through. He had to watch it as if he was fascinated to remind himself there was a world outside this too-intimate carriage and hope his senses would stop being so achingly conscious of her, in here with him. He didn't want to think about sensuous duets for lovers when he had another night of grinding frustration ahead of him and no end in sight.

'Oh, I see,' she said.

He heard the whisper of fine silk as she shifted on her side of the carriage as if she was uncomfortable as well, but it was unlikely to be for the same reason.

'She *is* an excellent musician,' she said and he might think she was jealous if his wife was that way inclined, but unfortunately she was not.

'True,' he replied shortly.

Even another wary silence felt more comfortable than talking about a lady he had hardly seen tonight while he was making such an effort not to stare at his own wife as if he was besotted with her. Tonight Georgia was dressed in a lavender silk gown that nearly matched the colour of her extraordinary eyes and the sad truth was she was the only woman he had ever seen through this haze of enchantment.

It was left over from the old days, he hoped. He had to tell himself so since she seemed as resistant to the idea of him as a man now as she was then. It was probably as well that fate had got between him and his plans to find a sweet-natured wife to settle down with her so he could forget Georgia as anything but an old friend, though, since beauty seemed to be purely Georgia-shaped for him.

Now he was confusing himself and he should stick to what was instead of wandering into fantasies of what might have been, if he was a lot luckier eight years ago. He couldn't regret marrying her now, despite this gnawing, endless hunger for a wife who said she wanted to want him, but couldn't quite manage to do so.

This wasn't the right time for him to imagine her eager and responsive to his endless desire for her in either of their wide and lonely beds. Unfortunately for him there was no right time for that yet, but he preferred to be bitterly frustrated in private.

'I was adding up how many tons of barley and oats we must keep for bread and reseeding in spring and what can be sold,' he admitted at last. He had better make sure he gazed at something inanimate next time he needed distracting from wanting his wife so ridiculously in public he dare not watch her instead.

'Oh, Max, that's probably sacrilege,' she chided him and was he fooling himself she sounded relieved? Probably, since he might as well be made of wood for all the notice she took of him as a man. Every time he tried to touch her she either jumped as if he'd scalded her or flinched away. 'You really must forget about the farms and Holdfast's doors and floors and windows now and again. You can't go around thinking about what needs doing there next every moment of the day.'

Why not? It stopped him thinking about her and how wrong he had been to think this devilish need would get easier to live with when his stupid sex realised it was not likely to be lucky any time soon.

Idiot! he raged at his merrily oblivious self before they were married.

They had been married over a month and every day had felt as if it was etched on his soul in a calendar of unmet longings that were eating away at it more deeply with every day that passed.

'I can listen to fine music with one ear and think about Holdfast at the same time,' he argued as if he had nothing much on his mind but his castle and crops. 'But I hope the musical Miss Stevens had no idea her playing wasn't holding my attention.'

'I suspect she was far too busy cursing me for snatching you out from under her nose to have even noticed that your mind was really elsewhere, especially as your brooding gaze was fixed on her for most of the evening as if you were fascinated by her.'

'I'm sure she has too much common sense to imagine that's true.'

'Why? There wasn't one man present tonight who could hold a candle to you for manly looks and presence and you have a castle to your name.'

'And a wife,' he reminded her dourly.

'Ah, yes, her,' she said with a sigh. His heart ached

as well as his much-tried manhood at the notion she regretted making those solemn vows to him as if she intended to keep them all one day. 'I am forever being congratulated on dragging you away from your precious castle and out into the wider world so you can socialise with your neighbours and I know you're only doing it for show. It makes me feel more like a well-trained sheepdog than the Lady of Holdfast Castle.'

'Well, you don't look like one if that makes you feel any better and I thought you liked being sociable. We are both expected to be so as newlyweds and I thought you were enjoying it.'

'As you don't like doing it, I shall soon grow weary of it.'

'Why? You didn't seem to suffer from ennui when you lived in London.'

'I did sometimes and that was different.'

'It was, wasn't it?' he said and heard the sarcasm in his own voice and sighed. 'We can talk about it in the morning, Georgia; we are both too tired to be sensible tonight.'

I have been too tired for that since we were married and now I'm bone-weary from not being able to sleep with you so close, but always on the other side of the sturdy oak door between our rooms. It is locked and we did put the key in your desk drawer the first night you became my wife in name only so you knew you could trust me to stay meekly in my place and not intrude on yours.

'We won't though, will we?' she argued, as if she was as frustrated with living in the same castle with him and them not being close as a man and wife should be as he was and that was highly unlikely. 'You will be up and away by the time I come downstairs tomorrow.

'You will come home to spend time with the girls before bedtime. Then we will dine with Leonora and maybe even your sister, before you spend the rest of the evening hammering away at some floor, or piece of panelling, or a window seat in another part of the castle so as not to wake the baby. You will be so tired after that you will go straight to bed and another day will have gone by without a chance for us to talk in private.'

'You should be glad,' he said shortly.

'Why?'

'Oh, for goodness sake, Georgia, use your head.'

'I have no idea what you mean,' she said with a sceptical sniff that said she knew perfectly well she was being awkward and irritating, but she wasn't going to stop it. If he was calmer and less tightly wound up in this endless, frustrated desire for her, maybe he would let himself hear the confusion under her offended reply.

As it was, he was much too tense to worry about her mixed-up feelings when his own were gnawing away at him so savagely. Thank heavens they were nearly home so he could get away from her before he blurted out needs that she didn't want to know about.

'It's best for us to be apart for as much of the day as we can manage without the wider world or your daughters noticing,' he told her, because she needed warning not to play with fire. 'I am just about civilised enough to accompany you on evenings like this as long as we keep to the terms of our agreement.'

'Do you hate me, Max?' she whispered as if she couldn't bring herself to say it out loud.

'Of course I don't,' he insisted brusquely and he didn't, not even after this endless month and several days of wanting and not being able to have his wife in his bed. 'I couldn't if I tried,' he added shakily and wondered if his life would have been easier if only he could.

As soon as the carriage halted outside the gate to the inner courtyard, he jumped down and waited for the steps to be lowered so he could hand her down from the neat carriage she had brought to their marriage as coolly as if they were polite acquaintances.

'I shall take a short walk before I retire,' he told her stiffly and walked away, pretending not hear her murmured question.

'Why?'

Because he had to. He had to stop himself from begging her to take him to her bed so he could please, please introduce her to the seductive arts and sensual pleasures she had no idea even existed at the moment and hope to slake at least some of this desperate pent-up passion at long last.

Chapter Ten

'Don't go, Max,' Georgia whispered to the late summer air, but her words were too quiet and too late for him to hear them and he wouldn't have listened anyway.

He was probably halfway to Holdfast village by now. She stood very still as she searched the shadows for a last glimpse of him before she gave up and went inside without her husband. If it wasn't for her stuttering heartbeat, and another unsatisfactory evening in his company, she might be able to enjoy the peace of the night so far from the nearest town or city.

She could hear the whooshing sound of swifts' wings as they flew over the parkland hunting for insects and sang their odd, keening music even in the dark. Then there was the distant call of an owl and the silence of small creatures frozen in fear. It was as well she was brought up in the country, she decided, or she might find the secret life of a late summer night eerie and disturbing and the bats gliding over the close-grazed parkland frightening. She might have, if all her attention wasn't fixed on her search for even a clue as to where Max had gone.

She was dressed for a polite soirée rather than for blundering through the sleepy countryside in the dark. Her fine silk gown and dancing slippers said no, even if the rest of her was reckless enough to want to chase after him to ask why he was being so gruff tonight. She probably didn't want to know and how far did Max mean to roam in *his* finely made evening clothes? She just hoped he didn't ruin them while he was out there doing whatever he was doing in the dark.

Or maybe he should. If he had nothing left to wear for evenings like the one they had just spent but his old working coats, he might refuse to spend more time as the newest husband in local society and save her the tension and tedium of being polite to his wealthier neighbours. There were too many sly whispers from ladies old enough to know better about what a very fine husband she had for comfort and the younger ones resented her for snatching the finest catch in the North Country out from under their noses.

What if Max had gone to find the besotted woman she had decided must mend his coats when she came here to confide in him all those weeks ago? Jealousy was like a physical force inside her and so hot and fierce it hurt her to imagine him tapping on the back door of a house secluded enough for her neighbours not to see him come and go to ruin his shadowy mistress's good name. He had no reason to keep his vows to his wife when she hadn't kept her side of the bargain.

Yet she had begun this evening with such hopes for more. She had almost meant it to be the one when she could say, *Yes, Max, come to me tonight and let's find out if I can lie with you and not hate it.*

Instead she had ended up hating Miss Stevens for being such a lovely paragon and now she was busy loathing a woman who might not exist. Would Max be as tense and terse with her if his sensual needs were being met elsewhere? He might if he felt guilty about it, she supposed gloomily.

She shivered and wrapped her arms around her waist in the darkness. If only he had stayed with her they could have wandered through the night together as they argued which stars were which the way they used to do as children.

They might even have been able to talk about when she might risk the intimacy of the marriage bed as her fantasies of making love with him were sneaking into her waking hours now. It felt as if she was being torn in two by her fear of intimacy and a fear just as strong that Max would give up on her and find solace in another woman's arms.

She sighed bitterly and finally realised the carriage had been driven back to the stable yard without her even noticing it go, so she was standing here like a statue of someone wistful staring after her absent husband. She sighed and went inside, feeling more confused than ever about her true feelings for the wretched man.

Taking her candle from a weary footman, she climbed the grand staircase alone and let herself into the grand old bedchamber adjoining Max's, but with that very significant locked door between them. He might as well sleep a mile away, she thought disgustedly, even if he was actually in his bedchamber instead of wherever he had gone instead.

Huggins had waited up for her and she undid Georgia's laces and unpinned her fashionable topknot, but seemed to sense her mood and helped her undress, brushed her hair and gently wound it into a loose plait for the night without comment. Georgia thanked her and told her maid not to get up early after such a late night. Then she jumped into her lonely bed before all the heat from the warming pan was gone.

What would it be like in the winter if she was shivering like this on a warm September night? But this was a different cold and there had only been a gentle hint of autumn in the air tonight when Max left her standing there like a fool as she stared after him. It wasn't a physical chill, it was loneliness. Max was probably sharing his warmth and passions with his mistress tonight and at least she would know exactly how to give him the comfort and joy his wife could not.

Georgia tossed and turned until her bedclothes made a tangled nest around her and sleep felt so far away she wished it was already day so she could get up again. With Max so firmly on his side of the door, when he was actually in his bedroom, it would hardly matter if she was wrapped in flannel and wool or a suit of armour since he would not be unlocking that damned door to get at her.

Night after night she had dreamt of him in here with her, making love to her and keeping her warm, but she didn't know how to be bathed and primped and wait for her lover with eager, shallow breaths and a fast-beating heart. This forbidden feeling of heat only he had ever aroused was burning at the very heart of her and it felt so uncomfortable she wasn't sure she wanted to feel more of it with him or not.

She didn't know how to flirt with serious intent or be eagerly responsive to a lover. She didn't want even Max to be here, expecting to put his sex inside hers and keep doing it until he rolled off her and went back to his own room to sleep while she stared sightlessly at the canopy of her bed and wondered why it was called making love. She glared into the darkness and cursed the memory of Edgar's selfishness. However often she tried to scour him out of her life, without Max here to keep him at bay, those hateful memories simply would not go away.

Georgia buttoned her nightdress all the way up to the neck and decided to forget Max as well for tonight. She wasn't going to listen for him sneaking home with the dawn after a tryst with the woman who mended his coats. Mrs Chilton was tired and needed her sleep so that in the morning she could pretend her husband had not marched away from her as if he could not endure her company a moment longer. She burrowed deeper down the bed so the feather mattress shaped itself to her body and never mind the cold side where Max never slept. She refused to cry over a man who had walked into the night as if she wouldn't even notice he had gone, but she had.

'Mama! Mama, where *are* you?' Millie yelled at the top of her voice and Georgia ran into the hall to see her daughter wringing her hands and pale as a ghost.

'Whatever is the matter, my love?' Georgia asked and felt her heart race with dread. 'Where is your sister?' she demanded sharply as all the terrors a mother could imagine made her shake with fear.

'Having a lesson on the pianoforte,' Millie said sulkily, but what a relief.

Now her worst fear had proved groundless, she could think properly and realised Millie should be doing something quiet in the schoolroom upstairs instead of sneaking out when her governess's back was turned.

'You have to come and please hurry, Mama,' Millie said. 'Please, it's Max, he really needs you!' she said tragically and looked as if she was struggling with something too hard for even an intrepid seven-year-old girl to cope with.

'What's happened?' Georgia whispered as she swayed on her feet and felt as if the world had stopped turning for a heart-stopping moment. Maybe this was her punishment for the shocking relief she had felt when Edgar was killed on the hunting field. She tried to ward off such an awful idea, but if Max was dead she knew her world could never be right again without him being part of it.

'He fell such a long way, Mama! Sam says he needs to be carried inside on a hurdle, but he sent Billy for the doctor and told him not to come back until he's found.'

'Where is Max, then, my love?' Georgia said, trying to sound calm for her daughter's sake.

It was like fighting an urgent force of nature as panic threatened to turn to hysteria for the first time in her life and that would make her no use at all. Logic said he must be alive if Sam had sent for a doctor. For the stoic groom who had been with Max for years to have insisted on one being fetched, he must think Max's injuries were serious, though, and Georgia felt as if her world was suddenly etched in black and white. Why hadn't she realised Max was the one who painted it in bright colours until now?

'He's in the old stable yards, but Sam wouldn't let me go near him.'

'Good, he should not have to worry about you escaping from your lessons yet again at a time like this. Now promise me you will go upstairs and find Miss Haverstock straight away. Explain what has happened as calmly as you can and try not to frighten your sister. Then you must wait for news because that's the kindest thing you can do for Max while I find out how badly he is injured.

'Go on, love; you have done what you needed to and told me about Max's accident. Now help me by staying with your sister and Miss Haverstock and I promise I will let you know how Max is as soon as I know myself.'

'Cross your heart?'

'Yes,' Georgia said. Millie knew Edgar had died from a crashing fall on the hunting field so of course she was afraid for Max, although she couldn't remember her father or how their life at Mynham had been before he died, thank heavens. 'Now off you go, and we shall have to talk later about the way you keep sneaking away from your lessons every chance you get.'

'I love Max,' Millie said as she turned to go quietly instead of making the usual excuses.

Georgia hoped her daughter really was going upstairs as she picked up her narrow skirts and ran outside as fast as her legs would carry her.

'So do I, Millie. Oh, so do I,' she found enough breath to murmur as she dashed down the steps to the stable yard to see what her husband had done to himself and if there was anything she could do to help him while they waited for the doctor.

She prayed as she had never prayed before that he would live. Her world would feel so empty without him she couldn't bear to even think about it. Why had she been such a fool about him for so long? She had only just realised he was the centre of her entire life and it could already be too late to do anything about it.

She dashed into the still derelict second stable yard and saw Max sprawled on the cobbles where he must have fallen and there was a broken ladder nearby to say why that was.

'Max! What the deuce were you *doing* up there?' she snapped in her shock at the risks he had taken by using such a broken-down old thing to climb up to the roof for whatever reason he had wanted to get there.

Now she knew what people meant when they said their heart had turned over in their breast with shock. It felt as if hers was doing exactly that before it raced on so hard it thundered in her ears with sheer terror for the injuries he could have caused himself and it came out sounding like fury.

She felt as if she would faint with terror if she let herself think too hard about what he must have done to himself falling from such a height and she just couldn't do that now. So she skidded to a halt beside him and fought for balance instead, since careening into his prone body would make things even worse. She managed to end up kneeling at his side by some wonder and peered down at him, feeling so helpless it was painful.

What could she do for him now she was here?

Tears knotted in her throat so she couldn't speak but she refused to let them fall. He looked as if he had more than enough to worry about without her weeping all over him as well. She wanted to feel all over his great, silly body for clues to which bits of him hurt the most and make sure he was still in one piece, but she knew it would do more harm than good. She winced at the very thought of hurting him more than he was already after falling from whatever height he had got to before the stupid ladder broke and sent the stubborn, darling man plummeting down on to the cobbled yard.

'Stable cat,' he muttered past a rueful grimace.

She wanted to weep again with relief because he still sounded like her Max despite whatever terrible injuries he had got climbing up that rickety ladder to rescue the stubborn old creature he was so inexplicably fond of. She let out her exasperation at him for giving her such a scare instead. 'Silly clunch,' she chided him.

'Me or the cat?'

'Both,' she said gruffly, clenching her hands into fists to stop herself patting and prodding him to try to tell where he was injured and doing more harm than good. 'Does your hand hurt?' she whispered as she eyed the closest one to her. She needed to feel his warmth against her skin so badly her own hand ached to hold it and maybe human contact would give him a little bit of comfort as well.

'Not that one,' he said and wriggled his long fingers invitingly as if to say, yes, he did want to feel her touch almost as badly as she did his.

'Good,' she said and gently took it in hers. The feel of his work-callused hand against hers made those stupid tears threaten again, but she sniffed hard and blinked them back before any fell on him and gave her fear away.

'Idiot,' she told him brusquely, but she clung to his hand as if she never intended to let him go again.

Maybe she shouldn't if this was what he did when he was out of sight. She hated to think this was her fault for being such a coward. She had never told him the thought of *him* in her bed was nowhere near as repugnant to her as she might have led him to believe. What if it was too late? What if he was hiding a terrible injury from her at this very moment? And she knew that was what the great, gallant idiot would do.

He made her heart race again by letting his pent-up breath out in a long sigh so she knew he was trying to cope with his pain without moaning and groaning. It was what he used to do when they were children and he got scratched or bruised, then tried to pretend it didn't hurt. Her heartbeat jarred again as her fear for his injuries threatened to outrun her faith in him getting better at the double as he always used to.

He was a strong man now, but she knew about the pain he was hiding from the very gentleness of his hold on her hand. His care and gentleness with her, even at a time like this, made her terror for him feel too big to hold inside, but he probably needed her to be calm. He didn't need his wife to fall into hysterics while he was coping with whatever he had done to himself thanks to his latest effort to avoid her.

'Can you feel your feet?' she asked.

Another burst of panic showed her a nightmare of him living without the power to move his legs or even the rest of the mighty body that was lying so worryingly still in front of her. The very thought of his frustration in that case made her feel sick, so goodness knew what it was doing to him. He was so active, so fiercely busy about this unexpected heritage of his. It would be such a restricted life if he couldn't stride about the place getting involved in every project he had started both here and out on the wider estate.

'Oh, yes. I can definitely feel them,' he said between his teeth, so he must have landed on them to make it such a stark effort for him to tell her so.

'Well, that's something, I suppose,' she said, then realised she was smoothing circles on his palm with her thumb without realising it. 'Sorry,' she said, trying to withdraw her hand in case she had hurt him.

He tightened it just enough to make her stop.

'Don't go, Georgia, don't leave me,' he murmured.

He must be feeling awful to ask her for comfort instead of offering it, as he always tried to if he thought anyone was in need of solace. Lord, now she was making him sound like a paper saint. He had never been one of those and never would be, thank goodness, because she could never live up to a saint.

'All right, I won't,' she said and, since her knees and back were hurting in this position, she shifted to sit next to him on the dusty old cobbles.

Once she was even closer to him, she managed to tear her gaze away from his face for a moment to see who else was here and what they were doing about him. She was just in time to see Becky race into the courtyard with her baby clutched to her shoulder as if the little mite was her talisman against more grief.

'Don't move him!' Becky shouted at the men Sam had gathered to carry Max inside on a hurdle. They were already looking uncertain about the idea as the Master of Holdfast was holding his wife's hand as if neither of them ever intended to let the other one go. 'The army surgeons used to say more damage was done by moving injured men than most of the wounds they had to start with,' she explained breathlessly to Georgia.

She nodded, thankful this wasn't the first time Becky had encountered an injured man and maybe she would be more use than Georgia felt she was being in Max's hour of need.

'I'll be all right in a minute…just getting my breath back,' Max muttered and Georgia met Becky's eyes in mutual exasperation.

He was trying to play down his injuries and Georgia could see the same fear in her sister-in-law's gaze as there must be in her own. She shifted her hand a little in the hope of making his feel less cramped.

'You won't be all right if you don't lie still and do as you are bid for once in your life, Maxwell Chilton,' she told him sternly. 'I shall send an express to your mother right away if you don't, because she might be able to keep you in order when the rest of us fail.'

'Dreadful idea,' he said ruefully, but he closed his eyes and shifted his hand so hers lay palm to palm with his. It felt like a bridge between his life force and hers and she wanted to pass him her strength and make him whole and well and not as badly injured as she dreaded him being after such a crashing fall.

'We need a cushion,' Becky demanded of the worried grooms and all the estate workers who had come running to find out how Max was as rumours of a catastrophe spread. Georgia must have looked puzzled by such an order after Becky had said they must not move him. 'For you, of course,' she added, as if Georgia should know she needed one without her help. For the first time she felt the strain on her legs and back as she leant over to hold Max's hand in a way that wouldn't jar his hurts.

'Oh, thank you,' she said and felt a little more optimistic when Max smiled faintly at the sound of his wife and little sister not being fearsomely polite to one another for once.

'Did you lose your senses?' Georgia whispered anxiously because how she and Becky got on didn't seem very important right now.

'Only over you,' he whispered back, the great fool.

'Be serious,' she demanded austerely.

'No, then,' he told her with a formidable frown that said he was still in pain, even if the fact he had not lost consciousness sounded promising to her.

'What happened to him, Sam?' Becky said as if she had given up on getting any sense out of her brother.

'I didn't see it happening, Miss Becky,' he said, reverting to the name he knew her by when they were younger. 'The stable cat was up there all night and Master Max said it needed to be brought down and it wasn't the cat's fault that the dogs chased it up there and it was too scared to come back down again. I was on my way back here with one of the good ladders when I heard the old one he must have found in the lumber yard crack. By the time I got here, he was already on the ground, swearing like a trooper.'

Georgia saw a faint burn of colour on Max's high cheekbones as she exchanged a hopeful look with Becky. If he had the energy to be embarrassed about his bad language, he might not be as badly hurt as they feared.

'Confounded cat,' Max muttered disgustedly. It felt wrong when the doctor hadn't even got here yet for her to decide he couldn't be in grave danger, but suddenly Georgia felt the most ridiculous urge to laugh at his gruff disgust with the cat and presumably himself for being taken in by it. There was no sign of the cross-grained old creature so it must have got down on its own.

'Remember they have nine lives next time and leave that confounded cat to come down when he's ready,' she chided him anyway. 'I shall have to make sure all the ladders for miles around are locked up safely so you can't get at them from now on unless you promise never to do that again.'

'You can have that one burnt first,' Max said grumpily and she let herself hope he had got away with sprains and bruises, although the bruising would be severe after such a fall.

'Here you are, missus,' the boot boy said. 'Lift up,' he added and shoved the cushion under her even as his mother scolded him for lack of respect from the front row of their audience.

'No, don't scold him; I am very grateful for it. Thank you,' Georgia intervened and was still shifting about to get comfortable without breaking contact with him when Max opened his eyes again and saw them all staring at him like an exhibit.

'What the devil are you all doing here?' he said in a stronger voice.

'Makin' sure you're still alive,' someone shouted from the back of the crowd.

'Well, I am, so you can all go away,' he ordered grumpily.

'Yes, get out of my way and let the man breathe,' a new voice ordered from behind them and Georgia sighed with relief as she recognised the physician from her adventures in local society.

'It doesn't sound as if there's anything very excit-

ing to see here if Mr Chilton is well enough to order
you back to your duties or your homes,' the doctor
added.

Georgia felt her heartbeat settle to something like
normal for the first time since Millie shouted for her
however many ages ago that was.

'Go on then, back to whatever you are supposed
to be doing,' Max managed to say wearily as the
crowd fell silent and watched the doctor survey his
patient. 'I don't want to moan and groan in front of
everyone for miles around.'

'Aye, he's well enough,' someone said.

Becky gave them her best *Why haven't you done
as you are bid yet, then?* look and they began to turn
away. Georgia wondered if Becky knew how much
she resembled her mother at times like this.

'Have they gone yet?' Max murmured and the
effort of sounding stronger must have taken its toll
since he held Georgia's hand more tightly as the doctor began to examine him as gently as he could.

'All except Sam and his cohorts and they never
do as they are told,' Becky told him with yet another
glare at the stubborn groom and gardener and estate
carpenters Max spent more time with than his wife
and Georgia tried not to resent them for it.

'We'll be needed yet, Miss Becky,' Sam replied
dourly and Georgia's euphoria because Max's colour
was getting better fell flat.

'True, you won't be walking anywhere for the next
week or two if I have anything to do with it, Chilton,

let alone climbing the stairs to your bed,' the doctor confirmed as he gently prodded one of Max's ankles. Georgia felt his flinch of agony even as he did his best to pretend it wasn't hurting.

When the doctor ordered his boot to be cut off and Max finally did moan, she shook her head as if she didn't have any sympathy, but held his hand even more tightly. She refused to let go of him even if he gripped harder in pain as Sam cut through the leather so carefully sweat stood out on his forehead.

Max could have been killed outright by such a fall, she realised as she looked at the broken ladder to distract herself from his pain and he wouldn't want her to cry on his behalf. Had he taken such a risk because he was too impatient to rescue the dratted cat or because he was driving himself so hard he wasn't capable of thinking straight any more?

The second, she decided and felt guilty all over again. Max was a man and she was his wife and he had all sorts of mature and manly needs she had been refusing to meet ever since they were married. Her deeply buried feminine instincts might want to, but she wouldn't let them.

Even the thought of her secret dreams of him rampant and lover like made her blush so fiercely out here in broad daylight that she hid behind her hair, which had escaped most of its pins during her frantic dash to get to him. Her breath was still tight in her chest with the terror of that dash and nothing felt the same as it had when she woke up this morning.

At last Max's boot was off and the doctor could examine his injured ankle. 'I dare say it hurts like the devil, but it's only a sprain,' the doctor said, but he frowned when Max shifted, then arched away from the cobbles with a yelp of pain he wasn't quick enough to bite back.

'And that sounds like a badly jarred back to me. You will have more bruises than you want to count in that case and the sooner they come out the better,' he added with a stern look to tell Max not to argue this was a fuss about nothing when he was so obviously in pain.

'I have got away lightly, then,' Max quipped and Georgia bit back a protest after the catalogue of injuries the doctor had been explaining to her as he went along.

'Tell me that when you want to tear around the countryside as if nothing is wrong with you and Mrs Chilton won't let you since I will have asked her not to politely, but very firmly,' the doctor argued sternly.

'I'm a busy man,' Max said as if he dreaded not being one and Georgia had to feel guilty again about why that was.

He sounded desperate to be back in the saddle so he could avoid her again, but there was very little either of them could do about his frustrations when he was being ordered to rest and she was supposed to make sure he did so.

'Not for the next few weeks you're not,' she told him severely.

'And if you won't listen to your wife you will have Mrs Sothern to deal with,' Becky said militantly. 'As I'm not as nice as Georgia, I really will send for Mama and she will make sure you can't escape our vigilance.'

'No, don't do that, she will be so worried about me,' Max protested.

'And we won't be?' Georgia said and raised her eyebrows at Becky as if silently asking if she agreed they would need the Dowager Lady Elderwood's help and never mind what Max wanted.

'Maybe you should remember *we* worry about you next time you try to rescue a cat that doesn't need rescuing,' her sister-in-law said and eyed the stable cat sauntering across the neglected old courtyard as if it had come to see what all the fuss was about. 'I shall make a furry waistcoat out of you if you ever pull a trick like that again, you miserable old bag of fur and bones,' she told the contrary animal as it rubbed against her caressing hand as if it knew she was as soft as her brother at heart.

'And I shall sew on the buttons,' Georgia told it sternly and it shot her a hard look as if it might even believe her.

Chapter Eleven

'Oh, for goodness sake, all you have to do is keep still, Max. Anyone would think I was getting ready to torture you.'

Georgia tightened her grip on the bottle of whatever it was the doctor said she needed to rub into his back and refused to go away again as he wanted her to.

'I will get Sam and the stable boys to come and hold you down while I rub this stuff in if you refuse to let me do it, so why don't you allow me to get on with it without all this fuss? You just need to take off your nightshirt and lie on your belly while I massage this stuff in because the doctor says it will bring your bruises out faster so your body can heal itself. The sooner we get this done, the sooner you can go back to sleep.'

'We men do have our own sort of modesty, you know?' he said grumpily and glared at her as if she was being perverse when she only wanted to help him get better.

She hated him having to lie up here hurting when there was something she could do to help him heal. She winced at the thought of rubbing the doctor's potion into his sore back and making it ache even more, but it would be cowardly of her to meekly go away without doing so.

She was his wife, for goodness sake—nobody should be better suited to do this than she was. If she must fight her inner coward to become a better wife to him, she was going to do so and she might as well start now.

'You should not have climbed a broken ladder to rescue a contrary old cat if you care so much about your privacy,' she told him unsympathetically.

She wanted to laugh at his grimace of offended manly pride, but bit her lip. He might refuse to stay in bed any longer if she let it out and that would undo all the good his first day of rest in a very long time had done him and do permanent damage to his magnificent but still injured body. Neither of them wanted that.

'He won't fool me like that again,' Max said gruffly 'and I don't need a noxious potion rubbed into my skin for no good reason. I heal quickly and I shall soon be up and about again without any help from that stuff.'

'No, you won't, the doctor said you must spend at least a week resting in bed and that's what you will do, even if we have to hide all your clothes so you can't get up. It's for your own good,' she added and his frown went even darker.

She went to pull back the sheets to get at his sore body whether he wanted her to or not. 'No,' he yelped and they tussled for a brief moment before she held up her hands and backed away, shaking her head at him in disgust.

'You are worse than my girls, but have it your own way. I always thought your mother should be told you have fallen and injured yourself,' she said cunningly and pretended she was off to send an urgent message to Flaxonby Dower House. She smiled when she got as far as the door and heard his horrified groan to say *no, that wasn't a good idea* and she knew she had won.

'Go on then, but don't blame me,' he said gloomily.

By the time she got back to the bed he had managed to whip off his nightshirt in record time and was lying face down on the bottom sheet with his head buried in his pillow and resistance in every line of his mighty and very male body. Her heart turned over at the sight of the bruises already marking his skin. She hated the thought of putting any pressure on places that already looked so sore, but if the doctor said this stuff would help him get better, she had to believe he knew what he was talking about.

Yet now she had got her way she wasn't quite sure what do with it. She eyed Max's naked back and flinched at the thought of feeling his warm skin and so much difference from her own much slighter frame under her massaging hands. No, she had to do this and it was high time she stopped being such a coward. This was to help him recover and she had promised herself yesterday she would do anything to bring that about.

She still winced as if she could feel the pain in his poor bruised back from here and no wonder he was being so cantankerous about it. She braced her shoulders and shook the bottle the doctor had handed her with instructions to use it and ignore her husband's protests he was perfectly all right and it was ridiculous to expect him to stay in bed for more than a day, let alone for the week it would take for him to be well enough to get up without doing himself some permanent damage.

'It smells surprisingly pleasant,' she said huskily. She heard her own mixed feelings about doing this in her voice and she didn't want him to know about them.

'Becky would probably do it, or what about Sam—he's used to rubbing his foul-smelling lotions and potions into the horses and swears he knows what he's doing.'

'To horses! And what kind of mother do you think I am not to know about rubbing whatever needs rubbing into my girls when they are ill or sore, Max?' she said and heard him sigh as if she was being ridiculous to even want to do this herself.

'I'm not a child,' he said as if she had offended

him yet again. 'But if you insist on doing this, please hurry up and get it over with,' he added and still refused to turn his head and look at her.

She frowned down at his tense back and poured a few drops of the oily, aromatic lotion into her palm, then rubbed her hands together to warm it while she gathered her courage and wondered which bits of him needed the healing stuff most. She gulped at the sight of so much muscular man laid bare for her wifely attentions and he sighed again as if he could read her mind and was trying not to think about them either.

'It isn't midsummer any more, Georgia. I will take cold waiting for this latest piece of unnecessary fussing if you don't hurry up,' he told her in a clipped but muffled voice that told her he was on the edge of sending her away and demanding Becky or Sam's attentions instead. She could not endure the thought of anyone else touching him as she should be and they would know it was because he could not endure her touch if she backed down now.

'Very well,' she said, but still started at the sensation of his vital warmth under her tentative fingers when she started on one of his shoulders. It seemed less intimate to begin there and she might gather more courage as she worked her way down his back and narrow hips to the tightly masculine backside beginning to show the worst of his bruises where most of his weight had landed when he fell. She muffled a gasp of shock at the feel of his heavily muscled shoulders so tense under her fingers.

'Please don't fight me, Max,' she murmured, 'this won't do any good at all if you resist my touch. The doctor said I must massage the stuff in as thoroughly as I could if it was to do your hurts and bruises any good.'

'Go on then,' he said, turning his head on the pillow just far enough to speak and give vent to a long-suffering sigh.

She felt him trying to let his muscles go slack under her fingers, but it didn't seem to be working. He felt so stiff and sore she massaged more deeply and thought she heard a muffled groan as the knots under her exploring fingers loosened while the rest of him seemed tenser than ever. She smoothed the stuff into his other shoulder, but it felt so awkward to lean across him to get both her hands on him and try to unknot the worst of his stiffness.

She frowned and tried to twist her body at a sharp enough angle, but his shoulders were so broad she had trouble even reaching his other one from this side of the bed. He felt so powerful as she tried to probe the tensest spots and soothe them with her probing fingers. She was so absorbed in learning the feel of so much masculine power under her massaging palms that she almost forgot why she was doing this and let out an approving little purr of satisfaction because there wasn't an ounce of extraneous fat on him.

Curiosity was threatening to take over from her fear and shyness and now she wanted to touch him with sensual intent and that wouldn't do at all! Even if she really wanted to do so he was in pain and all gruff and vulnerable and she had to fight such tenderness for him that it almost took her breath away.

For a choking moment she recalled the feel of Edgar's far less impressive body looming over her in bed as he took his pleasure and gave her none. She nearly flinched away from Max as her old fears threatened to overcome her concern for him, but a mighty shiver shook him from head to toe before she felt him force himself to go still again. Maybe he was cold and she pushed her bad memories aside because Max was the only man who mattered to her now and the only one who ever would. Edgar had no place in her life—he had no place anywhere now and she told his fading spirit he was not important and how bitterly he would have hated that fact.

She reached for the bottle again because she wasn't here to ask Max to teach her how to make love *with* him instead of enduring an act with nothing to do with love as she had to before. Maybe one day she could do just that—no, maybe she would quite soon—but it couldn't be today. She wasn't quite brave enough to want it to be now yet and he was injured as well as impatient to be up and away.

Time to concentrate on why she was here right now and that was for his benefit and not hers. She needed to forget about her dreams of them together in this bed with a whole night in front of them for her to learn about loving him as he deserved.

She made herself focus on the moment. Max's back was so heavy with muscle she could almost feel the hard work he had done for the last five years as he laboured to make his precious castle habitable and its estate almost prosperous again.

It felt so good to have an excuse to rub her palms over his taut skin and feel those mighty muscles with an approving hum, but she wasn't here to enjoy free access to his prone body, she was here to help him. All the same she silently approved of him working so hard and honing his manly body to the peak of perfection while he did so. She frowned down at his broad back while her hands worked hard to soothe his hard packed muscles into relaxation.

He had stubbornly refused to use her money to speed the restoration of this hardy old place yet, despite him agreeing to take some of it under their marriage settlements before they were married. He was still doing everything he could himself here and it made her feel like an outsider. She would have to argue harder when he was up to it again, but for now she shifted and fidgeted to try to get her hands on both sides of him at once, but decided drastic action was necessary.

'Have you finished?' he asked hopefully and she frowned.

At this rate she would have lines before she was thirty. 'No,' she said curtly, hitching her narrow skirts up so she could climb on to the bed without falling across his body and causing even more damage.

'What are you trying to do to me, Georgia?' he said with something like a groan of protest.

She closed her mind to the notion he had more to moan about than bruises and a potentially damaged back. She might be having fantasies about him in her dreams waking and sleeping now and this certainly wasn't going to stop her having some more, but she wasn't going to do anything about them while he was injured. It felt as if it might be her fault he had driven himself to exhaustion as well and that thought didn't sit comfortably with her.

'The sensible thing,' she told him as calmly as she could when it was an effort to get astride his legs without hurting him. The position felt so alien she almost wished she had finished as she got both of her hands on his body at last. 'Just lie still and be quiet,' she snapped as he seemed about to push himself up and away from her and the thought of all the damage he might do to himself seemed intolerable.

She managed to get her balance at last and fought a hollow feeling of insult and disappointment as she wondered why he didn't want her to be this close to him even when he was hurting and this could help him.

He had tensed as if she had jarred every ache in his poor body while she braced herself over his prone legs to try to get a better grip on his damaged body without putting too much pressure on his bruises.

She had been so careful not to hurt him that his unspoken resistance felt like a slap in the face.

'Easy for you to say,' he grumbled and turned his face away again so she couldn't see him frown.

She had to try to judge what was helping and what was hurting him from the play of his muscles under his satin-smooth skin since that was all he had left her to go by. She could only gauge the feel of them unknotting under her probing fingers to get a sense of whether this was working or not. Maybe the doctor was right, she decided, as some of them did seem to smooth out while others almost seemed to knot as she touched them.

'Apparently not so easy for you to do, though,' she said tightly. She reached for the bottle she had left as close to the edge of his night stand as she dared if it was not to fall off and she actually felt him moan this time. 'Did I hurt you?' she asked urgently and he felt so stiff and resistant maybe this was the wrong thing to do after all.

Perhaps she should have ignored the doctor's broad hints she should do this herself to make sure his patient could not just refuse to be helped by massage and his potions. Clearly the man was a good judge of character as well as a romantic and must think they were so recently wed that Max could not refuse her anything, but what did he know?

'No, I'm perfectly fine,' Max told the pillow on the side his wife should occupy if she had ever joined him in here. She had only come in here today for practical purposes, so why did that side of the bed seem like *her* rightful place when it was nothing of the kind?

'I will soon be done now,' she tried to reassure him.

She knelt up on either side of his long legs so she could put all her strength behind her hands and rub the slippery, oily liquid into his wide ribcage, the small of his back and his derrière, much sparser than hers.

Surely she didn't really hear him mutter, 'So will I…' into his own pillow as he tried not to arch in protest against her massaging hands while she worked on the most severely injured part of his anatomy.

Of course she knew he was a man and far less feminine touches than these were supposed to arouse them, never mind how they felt about the woman who was touching them. She stopped her massaging to gaze at his back, glistening with oil and whatever else was in this strong-smelling mixture. She was near the end of her self-imposed mission and felt a jag of disappointment she didn't want to think about as she ran her hands over his now glowing skin one more time.

She stayed where she was for a few tense, shamed seconds and wanted to run her sensually exploring hands over him while he was turned away from her and she could not read his thoughts and desires, or lack of them, in his dark brown eyes and react with tentative pleasure if he actually seemed to like it.

He was so different from her, so pared down and

muscular that she wanted to stay here and explore him in ever more intimate detail. But he was injured and that was a shameful idea. She leaned over him again and put her idle hands to work massaging in the last of the sharply aromatic liniment into his shoulders and pretending it was for his comfort and not hers.

It was hard not to let out a sensual moan of satisfaction as she felt his vigour and promise under her exploring, gently massaging hands again, but there was no good reason for her to keep them there. She had to use up far too much willpower to lever herself over him and get to the edge of the bed, then slither back down to the floor with an undignified shuffle it was as well he couldn't see.

At last her feet were on solid ground again and her skirts slipped down after her so she could reach for her shoes with her toes without even looking for them since she was still so guiltily fascinated by Max's prone body she couldn't take her eyes off him. She waited for him to say something since she couldn't think of anything sensible.

'Are you asleep?' she eventually managed to ask him and eyed the back of his head and the prone body he was holding so still it felt as if he was willing himself to be so if he wasn't already.

'Not yet,' she heard his muffled argument and almost wished he had pretended he was so she could slip away without saying another word.

'I will cover you up and leave you to it, then,' she

said uncertainly. 'If you keep the covers on and stay warm, I suppose there's no need for you to put your nightshirt back on.'

'No need at all,' he told his pillow, but didn't raise his head far enough to watch her tentatively raise the bedclothes until only his tousled dark hair was visible. 'Thank you, I might manage to sleep now,' he added from under them as she wriggled her feet into her elusive shoes and turned to go.

'The doctor said I was to do it twice a day,' she turned at the door to say.

'Sam can do it,' he said brusquely.

He turned on to the side away from her and drew the bedclothes into a protective cocoon so she felt she had no choice but to shrug and go away as he clearly wanted her to. He was so far from his usual vigorous self she didn't want to even think about how much he must be hurting. Maybe she should have left him to suffer in silence and ignored the doctor's orders.

Chapter Twelve

Max listened to his wife leave the room, at long last, and shoved his fist into his mouth to stop this stupid urge to call her back and beg to have her hesitant touch on his desperate body again, but this time with added sensuality. Somehow he managed not to and held on to his fragile self-control as she tiptoed out as if she really thought he was about to go to sleep.

He almost wanted to laugh at her naivety as he heard her close the door so gently behind her he might not have heard it if every sense he had wasn't so acutely aware of her. At least the ancient oak and iron door was solid enough to keep his no longer pent-up moan a guilty secret. He had to let the agony out so he wouldn't break down and yell for her to come back and drive him demented with her hesitant touch and bravery all over again and please, please could she be even braver this time.

If not for her courage in coming in here to do this for him when she clearly didn't want to touch any man as intimately as she had just touched him, he could not have resisted the magic of her hands on his naked skin and never mind the bruises she was so concerned about. She was so gallant and gentle with her shy touches on his aching body that he just couldn't turn over and let his wife see how rampantly aroused he was by her.

His absolute need was painfully obvious to him and of course he wasn't flinching away from her pressure on his bruises, but from his own reaction to her hesitant, gentle hands on his bared back. His outward hurts felt so little compared to the old familiar ache of this endless need for her and her alone. He wanted his wife—in his bed, being his delicious and delightful lover in the glorious privacy a man and wife should have by right. No, not by right—because it *was* right and it felt right and they both wanted it so badly.

He groaned as that fantasy brought him sharply back to the brave part of her visit, because she had to put aside her past experiences in order to do this for him and it felt so touching he could almost weep for both of them. The confounded, interfering doctor must have told her she was the best person to do the job and he supposed the man would assume they were intimate whenever the need took them as they had been married such a short time.

It would only take him one knowing glance at Max staring at his wife during any of the social gatherings they had been to lately to see how much Max wanted to make love to his beautiful wife. It wasn't fair to blame the doctor for not knowing he wanted Georgia with every fibre of his being, but she was so afraid of such intimacy he hardly dared touch her, let alone try to make love to her.

It was Max's constant battle to fight and the gap between his needs and hers had been torturing him since they were eighteen years old so he should be used to it by now. He groaned again as the force of that need rode him like an angry tiger and he wasn't used to it at all and knew he never would be.

He rolled himself into an aching ball and never mind the doctor's orders to lie flat just in case his back was injured more than he thought. The man didn't know about his current patient's worst hurts as they were usually so well hidden. They were not caused by his accident, but by what Jascombe had done to Georgia.

Yet she had still come here to try to help him in the teeth of her fears of being so close to a man. Hope almost blotted out his aching, driving need for a moment, but he knew it was dangerous. He groaned into his mistreated pillow and tried to cling to it anyway. Georgia's tentatively exploring touch on his desperate-for-her body had lit some of it in him, but he knew he couldn't take such temptation again without his control snapping.

Somehow he would put more chains on his frantic inner lover to get them into this bed as truly man and wife one day, but he had to be patient. A little hope still felt dangerous as he closed his eyes to will his overactive imagination to sleep and, please, please, take his aching body with it.

For a week the doctor insisted Max stay in bed as the bruising came through with a depth and darkness even he was shocked by when the exasperated man held up a shaving mirror to show him how bad it was. He argued he had taken a far worse beating eight years ago and time had healed him then so it was sure to do so now.

News of his old injuries only got him a deeper frown from the doctor and the insistence he must lie as still as a log to make sure any jarring of his past injuries had healed properly as well as all the new ones. After a whole week of lying still and being unable to avoid the sweet torture of having Georgia nearby day after day, he felt both racked by it and privileged to have had so much of her company.

Since Max was such a gentleman nowadays that he had to dress like one far too often, she had accepted his compromise that the footman recently promoted to be his valet would massage the dratted liniment into his back. At least the ordeal of having Georgia do it had not been repeated, although she still came to his room to sit with him as if she craved his company nearly as much as he did hers, but that seemed very unlikely when she never had before.

He could not read for more than a few minutes without his arms aching from holding the book above his head while he was laid flat as ordered, so Georgia and Miss Haverstock had taken it in turns to read to him whenever they could spare the time. Miss Haverstock had a fine contralto voice and a gift for reading aloud, but it was Georgia's voice he listened to as if he was spellbound. He was. He loved the sound of her voice.

She could recite a laundry list and he would be enthralled, but sharing a book they would usually have read alone felt intimate. They enjoyed the witty and the sublime in poetry and drama together and sharing their thoughts and opinions made him listen even harder in order to keep up with her when she stopped reading. It made a good distraction from the frustration of lying still as if he was made of stone while she sat so near to him with never a lover-like word said between them, except the ones they borrowed from poets musing or raging about their favourite subject.

It was as well the girls would burst in whenever they could escape their lessons or their nanny so he couldn't risk saying anything personal to their mother and driving her away. Millie and Helen would sneak into his room with such furtive looks around it first to make sure their mama wasn't about to tell them off that it was hard for him not to laugh at their antics. He should feel guilty about letting them stay, but they did lighten the long days of inactivity with their chatter about the world outside and whatever they were supposed to be doing instead.

In the end Georgia said they could make a brief visit to his room after breakfast and then they must learn their lessons until Miss Haverstock said they were over for the day. Then they would be allowed to join him again until it was their bedtime.

Max looked forward to evenings when Georgia sat by his side of the bed sewing, if she wasn't joining in with their games or having to settle one of their arguments. They felt like a family and he hadn't realised how much he wanted one of those until Georgia and her daughters had come to live at Holdfast. He wasn't even going to think about them adding to that family until there was some chance of it actually happening.

At last he was declared fit to get up again, although he was still not supposed to busy himself with his castle and lands until he was declared completely well. He let his valet dress him for once and warily stretched his long body as soon as the lad was done. Max decided he felt almost ready for anything now and never mind what the doctor said to the contrary.

He strode around the room a few times to make sure his legs were working properly and realised how much this last week had changed things. Despite the endless frustration of sleeping in the bedchamber next to Georgia's and hoping she would use the key in the locked door between them one day soon, life felt good.

He had lived here alone for so long and felt so alone

when Georgia was married to Jascombe before that. He had almost forgotten how it felt to be part of a family and now he wanted to be at the centre of this one, with his wife. It was time he took another risk and told her how much he wanted her, even if she didn't want to hear it yet. She had to know, had to be told how unique and lovely and desirable she was, because Jascombe had nipped away at her belief in herself so often she didn't seem to know it.

It was going to be Max's pleasure to keep letting her know she was beautiful and clever and endlessly desirable. She had never had an adoring lover before. She didn't know how it felt to be loved, so he would just have to keep telling her she was lovable and exactly right as she was when he could persuade her to listen.

There was no need for her to change anything about herself to make her his perfect lover. If they got no further into the kind of marriage they had promised to strive for than that, he would know he had done everything he could to wipe away Jascombe's vile mistreatment of her and make her feel she was worth loving.

'There you are at last,' he said when he tracked her down to the sitting room in the Tudor wing she had made her own.

He sat down in a chair facing hers as if he was weary from the effort of getting dressed and walking downstairs, when he was really tired of resisting this gnawing ache for her as his lover day after lonely day.

'How do you feel?' she asked.

He must still look pale and interesting since she hadn't muttered an excuse and rushed off to do something else now he was up and about and might be dangerous again. He glanced at her sewing and realised she was mending one of her daughters' aprons. That seemed rather touching when she could employ a sewing woman to mend it or make new ones rather than bother with them herself.

'Stupidly unsteady after spending a week in bed like an invalid,' he said ruefully.

'You *were* injured,' she told him as if he might not have noticed and he caught her furtive glance at him sitting here pretending to be weak with the effort of getting downstairs to say she wasn't convinced he should be up even now.

Or was he safer when he was in bed laid out flat and seemingly helpless? He understood the fears behind her hesitancy about him being up and about, but somehow he had to break through the barriers she was putting up between them again if they were ever going to be any closer to husband and wife than they were right now.

'I was nowhere near as badly hurt as everyone seemed to think I was,' he said blandly and decided even what she thought was a dull and practical grey morning gown was a foil for her startling loveliness and he was still surprised by it at times.

'Hmmph,' she murmured disapprovingly and went on with her sewing.

The morning sun brought out the shining gold and red lights in her russet curls as if they had a life and fire of their own. Thank goodness she had left off the ridiculous cap she sometimes wore. She said she was a matron now and not a girl, but leaving it off felt like her shedding at least some of her cares.

He had given her a lot more when he fell off a ladder, but he couldn't regret it now he didn't hurt as much. That clumsy fall had changed things between them and they were closer now than they had been since they ran wild round the Yorkshire Dales together as children. Not close enough, but closer was good.

Yet Georgia was still so self-contained he fought to understand her at times. He was having to gauge her true feelings from quick flickers of emotion in her eyes, or a gesture she would swiftly control again. Those were enough to say the real Georgia was still there under the armour she hid behind during her wretched first marriage.

He had best not think about Rat Jascombe when he was trying to coax more of the old Georgia out in the open and maybe that could be enough for now. Perhaps this wasn't the right time to challenge her with his lustier desires. It felt peaceful and domestic and almost content in here and that felt like new hope to him.

It was precious to a man who had lived without any for so long. The old depth of feeling he had learned to hide so well threatened to drown out caution and good sense, but he walled it up again. He tried to look tame and hoped she would go on sitting there instead of bolting out of the room to find something she had to do on the other side of the castle.

Sometimes she was as good at avoiding him as he was her. He had to stop doing it and try to convince her she was valued and secure and maybe even loved instead and this seemed a good place to start. Then perhaps she would feel like more like the grown-up version of the impulsive, adventurous, hopeful Georgia she had been before Rat Jascombe undermined her.

'We had to make sure there were no hidden injuries and you could have been hurt so badly, Max,' she said as if she had been working up to saying something wifely while he was deciding what to do next. 'Promise you won't work so hard that you get so tired you can't think straight and rescue cats that don't need rescuing?'

'I can't. I need to work,' he said and he did, but being so abrupt about it wasn't going to get them anywhere. 'You know how much I have always hated being idle,' he added with a smile that invited her to share memories of their adventures when he was a restless boy and she was almost as bad.

'I do remember you driving your mother nigh mad with your restlessness on wet days when we couldn't play outside,' she said and they shared memories of the more inventive ways they thought up to pass the time on rainy days as children for a while.

If they ever managed to be lovers, they would have a lifetime of knowing one another to build on. He felt the lovely promise of being her best friend again as well as her lover and it was worth waiting for, just not for ever.

'Promise you won't tell Millie and Helen what we used to get up to when we were young, Max,' she said with a smile that did things to his willpower if only she knew it, but she clearly didn't or she wouldn't be doing it.

'Aye, I don't think my nerves would stand it if they copied some of our wilder starts,' he said. He shuddered at the thought of what two enterprising little girls might get up to with a whole castle to work with. 'They are very like you were when we were growing up,' he added with a smile for her daughters as well as the memory of how intrepid she was as a girl. 'You can't help liking them, can you? They can be such tricky little devils I sometimes wonder why, but they are still rather wonderful.'

'They love you,' she said with a challenge in her eyes as if to say *And don't you dare deny it*. 'I'm glad they have you as well as me now and you love them, too.'

'I will always be the best stand-in father I can to them, I promise you.'

'You don't need to, Max. I know they couldn't have a better one than you.'

'Thank you,' he said gruffly to hide his feelings this time.

He hadn't realised how protective a father felt about his girls until Georgia's daughters dropped into his life and he wanted to make sure they had happy and fulfilled lives from that moment on. He was going to be a formidable obstacle in the way of any young man who wanted to marry one of them—and they had better have marriage in mind or be ready to face his sternest fury as well as their mother's.

They sat in silence for a while, but it felt easy, almost domestic as she sewed and he brooded about eager young men and how to make sure they knew he was up to every lusty thought in their mistaken young heads, even if it would be a decade or more until he had to glare at any for having wrongheaded ideas about his adopted daughters.

'Would you ring the bell for coffee, please, Max? Since you think tea is only fit for the cat to lap, you might as well drink it here with me so I can keep an eye on you—not that the villainous old cat you went to all that trouble to rescue is ever going to get the chance to develop a taste for it,' she said with a frown for the cause of his injuries.

He felt a fool for taking the ragged old tom's wails to be got down from his perch seriously, but as it led to here and now Max was a lot more willing to forgive Tom Cat for his play-acting than she was. Max drank his coffee while she moved on to darning a rip in one of Millie's favourite gowns and he was feeling lazy and almost contented when she jolted him out of his mellow mood by remembering he had not agreed to do much less from now on.

'Promise me you won't work as hard in future, Max?'

He thought about it, but there didn't seem much point in lying about his frustration any longer. 'No, I can't stop being busy,' he told her abruptly.

'Why? It's not as if you need to be land steward, master builder and carpenter's labourer all rolled into one now you have got the estate running as it should be again.'

He was glad she didn't mention her money sitting in the bank waiting for him to employ a steward, foreman of the works and a lot more labour than he could manage. 'I need to carry on working hard, but I promise not to let a contrary old cat fool me again.'

'But why, Max? You don't need to do everything yourself any more and we need you to be here with us at least some of the time.'

'I can only stop myself begging you to be my wife in more than name every time I catch you alone by making sure I don't have much chance to do so,' he admitted at last.

He felt hot and a little ashamed of that lack of self-control and his pulse raced as she went as still as a statue with shock that he had said it out loud. He had to meet her gaze because he needed to know if she still flinched from the very thought of him so rampant for her. Except it turned out she was too good at disguising her emotions for him to tell.

'Oh,' she said, looking flustered, but not as revolted as he had dreaded.

'So, I shall take the rest of today to get my legs working properly again, then get back to being as busy as I can be with everyone stopping me to say I must be careful,' he tried to joke.

It felt as if he had thrown a grenade into the quiet contentment of this room she had made her own and she was waiting to see if it was going to explode. He might as well go and hack at something in the still overgrown parts of the gardens, since he had promised not to leave the castle today. He had already been told that Madam had hidden his carpentry tools until she deemed him well enough to use them.

'I want you too, Max,' she shocked him by saying so softly he thought he must have misheard. 'I want to be a proper wife to you,' she added, so his astonishment must be showing.

'Because my accident shook you and you are feeling guilty,' he said flatly. 'I know you, Georgia. Don't you dare sacrifice yourself to stop me riding off my frustration until I'm so tired I don't care if the very idea of being intimate with me repulses you any longer.'

'It wouldn't be a sacrifice, or repulsive because it would be you. I want to want you so badly, Max. I'm almost sure I already do.'

'I'm still me, Georgia—an older version of the silly boy who couldn't say how much he loved you all those years ago.'

'Is that really all you think you were to me back then? A tongue-tied boy?'

'Yes, and I would have walked over hot coals if you asked me to, but I couldn't find the words to tell you so and look what that led to. It's all still there inside me, Georgia. The heat and desire still simmering like molten lava, searching for a way out, and, however brave you are, I don't want you as a duty or a sacrifice or to stop me having another stupid accident.'

'It was a *very* stupid accident,' she told him severely and if this wasn't such a serious conversation he would laugh.

'It was, but I was a fool to think we could live cheek by jowl while I waited for you to want another child and you are such a good mother I thought you were sure to sooner or later. I can't tell you how much I yearn for it to be mine, but I should have found another way to protect you and the girls from Ness's folly.'

'Stop being so annoyingly noble, Max, and listen to me properly. I want to be your wife. And, yes, I do what another child because it will be yours. But if you're never here, how am I ever going to get used to the idea of wanting you as I want to want you?

'I want *you* too much; I'm not safe.' He gave up sitting still and paced restlessly to the window to stare blindly out of it as he searched for the right words. 'I have to be busy and wear myself out so I won't beg or get carried away.'

'Oh, Max, what a confession, but I will trade you one for it. I have been having very peculiar dreams about you,' she said with a guilty look. 'And lately they have got even more peculiar,' she added with a fiery blush so he guessed they were at least bordering on the erotic and tried not to preen at the thought that he was her fantasy lover.

'When did they start?' he asked casually.

'Soon after we were married,' she said as if she was confessing to a crime.

'And when did they stop?'

'They didn't,' she said. 'They haven't,' she added and refused to look at him directly.

'And you find them shocking?' he probed carefully.

'Very much so, but today I will confess to finding them rather intriguing as well.'

'I'm so glad they are of me, then,' he said unsteadily and he was. In fact, he was delighted, but he had to be careful not to sound too much so when she looked so dubious about having them.

'I didn't know dreams could be so wild.' She heaved a weary sigh, as if fighting not to dream of him had disrupted her sleep.

'Dreams can do what they like, it's why they are called dreams,' he said gently and she made a wry face.

'Mine certainly do,' she told him grumpily and he had to smile.

'Why don't you tell me more?'

'I can't,' she said with a shuffle in her chair to say this was embarrassing.

'Coward,' he accused her softly.

'Yes, and I wish I was the Georgia in those dreams for your sake, but I'm this one. A dull and boring woman you rashly married and in real life I'm just a scared rabbit always running away from what we could be if I wasn't so stupid.'

'You're not dull or boring, or a rabbit. You're so wrong about yourself it's almost funny,' he said to hide the fury roaring through him because Jascombe had made her think all that rubbish about herself.

'You are the trickiest, most complicated, fascinating, infuriating and truly beautiful woman I have ever met. You intrigue me, Georgia, you always have done and always will do. Don't shake your head as if you think I'm flattering you, because I'm not and you know I'm not a smooth-tongued seducer. I'm not a smooth-tongued anything if it comes to that, just a blunt north countryman who can't get the right words out at the right time.'

'I love your plain speaking when you actually get round to it. Edgar had all the right words, but he didn't mean any of them. He begged me to marry him or his life would be blighted for ever.'

'Sometimes I wish the Rat was still alive so I could pound him to a pulp for what he did to you, but since you would still be married to him if he was then I'm delighted he's been in his grave for five years.'

'So am I,' she said and met his eyes at last.

'And I'm even more delighted now you are married to me instead,' he said and saw the true Georgia she had always been at heart in her steady gaze. 'You are magnificent, Mrs Chilton,' he added and it was no good, he just had to kiss her even if it sent her scrambling for the barricades.

At least she didn't flinch this time. She even fitted herself closer to him as he kept his mouth light on hers with a stern effort of will. It would have been just a quick caress, lip to lip, if not for her taking a shaky breath and running a wondering hand across his cheek with a hum of interest that sounded almost like a purr.

He couldn't stop himself deepening his kiss as the sound of it made hunger lick inside him, but he didn't want to frighten her. Panic turned somersaults with hot need inside him. If she hated his kiss as much as she had Jascombe's, it would kill a part of him. She gave an odd little whimper and pushed her body flush with his and he was so relieved he huffed out an unsteady chuckle against her mouth and felt her misunderstanding it as she stiffened with offended pride.

'Not laughing at you,' he murmured in the bare minimum of space between them it took to say anything at all. 'Hysterical, with joy,' he added and with a great sigh went back to kissing her as if both their lives depended on it.

Chapter Thirteen

Georgia felt the tremor in his work-roughened hands as Max explored her face with gentle fingers and even kissing wasn't enough touch after all these years apart. He was her dear friend, her Max, yet he was the lover she had dreamed of as well. She had to stop letting him take all the weight of their marriage on his shoulders and kiss him back.

His mouth became more demanding and she stopped caring about who was kissing who. The heat inside her was fierce as his tongue made little forays at the gap between her lush lips where her breath was coming short and shallow, so she opened it wider and felt his tongue exploring deeper. The fire inside her was so hot and sweet she wanted to moan and whisper a demand for more, but their mouths were too urgent to make words.

She had feared this much intimacy with Edgar, felt so choked and invaded. She stopped breathing altogether for a moment, but sly little darts of temptation seemed to reach down to the very heart of her femininity at the touch of Max's tongue on hers so she forgot about Edgar altogether.

Stories about heat and passion and delight she had never even heard before spun around in her head and made her heartbeat race. She heard a soft murmur of extreme pleasure and realised it came from her.

Max was raising his mouth to ask her questions about her first real kiss, if she excluded that teasing, butterfly one on their wedding day, and she didn't know the answers, so she kissed him this time, echoing his moves back at him because they were the only ones she knew. She tried them out and felt Max trembling with need and it felt so powerful that she nearly got carried away.

It felt novel and shocking to make him gasp, to hear and feel his breath coming short because *she* was kissing *him*. Then he deepened the kiss with a moan and for a tense moment she felt invaded as his tongue pushed fully between her lips and past her teeth this time and he probed the privacy inside. Edgar threatened to push his horrid possession of her and break this lovely rightness, so she fought against the shoddy past. This was Max and she knew he would never hurt her.

'Max,' she murmured as he raised his head at the sound of her gasp of almost protest at the heat raging inside her with nowhere to go.

She went up on her tiptoes to grab their kiss back

so Max was too occupied to reply. She heard his groan as she made funny little noises to say kissing him tasted delicious and he needed to know it. Maybe he was right and she could be good at this kind of loving, with him. Then she was disgusted with herself for thinking there would be marks given out for method and performance afterwards.

All that mattered was them as their kiss went deeper and more desperate and she was plastered against his body like a second set of clothes. Siren Georgia from her wild dreams took charge and stretched sinuously against his powerful male body as she let out a soft moan of something deep and yearning that sounded so strange to her.

She heard Max suck in a great breath as if it was the only way he could hold back from kissing a lot more of her than just her throat from ear to collarbone as he left tender little licks of fire all the way down it. His kiss settled on the racing pulse at the base of her throat and his mouth was so hungry and hot and eager she moaned again and would probably have done a lot more if the door hadn't burst open so Millie and Helen could dash in.

Seeing their mother locked in Max's arms, they stared at them as if they couldn't believe their eyes. They were dumbstruck for a few blessed seconds while Georgia tried to reshape herself into being their mother again and not Max's would-be lover.

'You're up at last, Max,' Helen burst out in her

usual headlong fashion when she was excited, or worried.

'Nobody told us,' her big sister added suspiciously.

Max let Georgia go with a haste that made her feel cold and alone, but what else could he do with two pairs of accusing eyes on him?

'You two were kissing each other when we came in, weren't you?' Millie accused as if she had caught them playing with fire and Georgia thought she might be right and the trouble with fire was it left only ashes behind it.

'None of your business, young lady,' Georgia made herself say briskly and where she found enough brisk from goodness only knew.

'You were, though, weren't you? You can't pretend you weren't when we saw you hugging and kissing one another and now you've both gone red.'

'What if we were, Minx?' Max said smoothly. He had got himself under control again a bit too swiftly, hadn't he?

Georgia didn't want him to be controlled with her and, considering she was having second thoughts about the more she had practically begged him for only moments ago, that probably made her almost as contrary as her daughter.

'Yuk! Grown-ups who kiss like that have babies.'

'Do they?' Max said as if fascinated by the very idea and Georgia had to smile and forget how serious they had just been together.

Of course her girls loved him, why wouldn't they?

He always took their odd questions and funny little ways seriously and didn't treat them like idiots just because they were too young to know some things she wasn't quite sure about herself, like the difference between loving and just wanting.

'I'm not entirely convinced by your theory, but what's wrong with babies if we did happen to have one?' he asked lightly.

Georgia thought he was every bit as serious and every bit as worried about their response to the idea as she was now. He didn't know she badly wanted to have his child one day, but she didn't want her daughters to feel left out if she did. She blushed at the very thought of what they still had to do together to make it a possibility and avoided his eyes.

'People want them more than us,' Helen chipped in with a nod to say it was true, so there was no point trying to tell her she was just a little girl who didn't know things.

'Which people would those be? I don't see any of them in this room,' Max said lightly. Georgia could see the anger in his eyes as he guessed who 'they' were before Helen confirmed it, but she knew he would hide it in front of them.

'Grandpapa Duke and Uncle Chert and the servants, except Cook; she liked us.'

'Are they here, then? *I* certainly didn't invite them.'

'Neither did I,' Georgia murmured, secretly vowing never to do so.

Max gripped her hand as if he knew what she was

thinking and the warm contact of his against hers stopped her falling back into a false world where heirs were all that mattered and girls were barely tolerated by their own kin. She didn't belong in that world now, she never had, and she squeezed his hand to say how delighted she was to be living in this one.

'If you two have a baby, he could be a boy and then you wouldn't want us,' Helen persisted as if she was telling them facts they ought to know already and no five-year-old child should ever have to think that was how their life was going to be.

'What do you think, Max?' Georgia made herself say lightly even as her heart broke for her precious children kept at Mynham for three whole weeks without her to counter the stupid Jascombes' stupid obsession with their stupid male heirs. 'Shall we keep them? Obviously they *are* girls and they can be noisy and naughty and occasionally they get very dirty. Sometimes they smell a bit as well and even I don't want to hug them then and I'm their mother.'

'I think we might as well, since nobody else would want to and boys can be even noisier and dirtier and a lot smellier. Maybe they are going to teach any baby brothers and sisters who do happen to come along to be almost as much of a nuisance as they are, but I think we might risk it, if you're game, my dear?'

For a moment Millie looked deeply offended, then she saw the smile in Max's eyes as he pretended to be serious so she pulled a hideous face at him instead. 'You don't deserve us,' she told him. 'Not me, anyway; Helen loves her doll more than anything else in the whole wide world so she won't care what you think of us for very long.'

'I don't, I really and truly love Max,' Helen argued and they were in mid-quarrel about who loved him the most when Leonora came to fetch them back to the schoolroom. She had a stern look for their parents as well as her reluctant pupils this time to say why weren't they doing it for her, since these two scamps were their children and they were supposed to be responsible adults.

'Thank you,' Georgia said shakily as they heard her daughters arguing all the way back upstairs and Leonora's quiet rebuke they should not have run away from their lessons, even if Max was up and about and they wanted to see him standing on his own two feet again.

'For kissing you almost in public in the middle of the day?' he asked her with a wry smile she didn't quite know what to make of.

'No, for making light of the Jascombes' stupidity and showing their ridiculous obsession with male heirs doesn't matter and our girls are wonderful. I want to spit roast my former father-in-law and brother-in-law over a slow fire. They made my girls think they are of no account while my back was turned.'

'Their loss and you had better let me tie the knots because you were never any good at them and we wouldn't want them to get away,' he said. And there he was—her man, her real history, the crucial part of her family she never wanted to live without again.

'No, we would not,' she said and laughed as he meant her to. 'Oh, Max, whatever would I do without you?' she asked and tried not to be disappointed when he just grinned and went off to discuss something urgent with the estate foreman instead of taking up where they had left off before the girls interrupted.

Max kept Georgia on the edge of something wonderful for days after their first real kiss with a sensual touch here, a fleeting kiss, or an unsatisfying caress when nobody saw him touch her, but she felt it long afterwards as if he had branded her. Her inner sensualist was so frustrated and the rest of her so impatient with this feeling of being slightly off balance all the time.

She would lie in bed at night, wishing she had enough courage to use the key he had given her on their supposed wedding night so she could tumble straight into something new and slightly dangerous with her lawfully wedded husband. At least then she could join him in his grand bed every night instead of being lonely and restless in her own grand one.

So many times she had got up, wrapped herself in a fine woollen shawl, since it was now early autumn and this was Northumberland, and stood on her side of the sturdy ancient oak planks, trying to work up enough courage to open it and step through into them being Mr and Mrs Chilton and truly husband and wife at long last.

She usually got as far as touching the cool old metal handle before her doubts set in and stopped her turning the key she now kept in the lock, waiting for her to find enough bravery to turn it and breach the promise he had made her that first day here: that he would never open it first and demand what she didn't want to give freely.

That sensual kiss with Max the first day he was downstairs again had taught her to want him so much. Then he had confused her day after day by trailing barely there kisses along her bare arms, or there would be a swift brush of his lips on her bared shoulder when she was wearing evening dress. Maybe even one on her cheek in passing as he placed her evening cloak around her shoulders, if she was lucky. Then he would walk away; leave her shivering with, well, something warm and mysterious she didn't fully understand yet.

He also left small presents in unexpected places to remind her that she was very much a woman nowadays and maybe she could dare to be a sensual one with him again very soon? She would, if she could only let herself believe she was truly that woman deep down.

First, Max gave her a delicate silk shawl so finely made she was sure it would pass through her wedding ring if she ever took it off to find out. The feel of the light-as-air stuff against her bare skin on nights when they had ventured out to meet local society made her shiver with such delicious consciousness of her own body. It was almost as if Max was touching her instead of the luxurious fabric.

She was almost sure he had picked it to remind her how much he wanted to slide his fingers wherever the silk lay and maybe kiss her there as his touch went sensuous and never mind what local society thought of them if they stayed home to play instead of going out that night.

His eyes had been so hot with desire when he adjusted it against her skin as they walked up the steps tonight she had shivered with hot longings she still didn't fully understand. She hadn't dared to wear the perfume in public that he had left in a finely made glass phial inside her sewing table, since she didn't want to be considered fast.

But on nights when she wanted to open that door between their bedchambers so badly she shook with it and turned coward yet again, she would sniff its heady promise of sensuality and dab a little on the pulse point where he had kissed her so hotly that day, just to remind herself she *would* be his lover one day and it was going to be worth fighting her inner demons for.

The sweet heat at the heart of her felt dearly, tortuously familiar now. She knew he was doing his best to stoke it into a blaze high enough to sear away her old terror of being intimate with a man and she smiled secretively at the thought of the tempting, clever, sensual lover her oldest and dearest friend had grown up to be and never mind if he did think he still wasn't very good with words.

She knew he was wooing her without them, teaching her things about herself even her wanton inner dreamer never thought about feeling until now. Why had she never dreamt Max would be such a cunning lover? It made her blush to even think of what he might do in real life when her dreams had grown wilder every time she turned away from that dratted door and headed back to her bed to dream of what she didn't dare do with him quite yet.

The next morning she frowned down at the delicate pendant Max must have persuaded Huggins to place on the tray with her morning chocolate. It wasn't that she didn't like it, she loved it. The elegantly made and satin-lined leather box was like a present in itself. Of course she was too weary to get out of bed early and breakfast with everyone else after she had spent so long with her hand on that wretched key last night it was nearly dawn by the time she finally gave up and now she felt… Hmm, how did she feel? Utterly bewildered, yet so enchanted at the same time she was breathless and shivery.

She stared down at her lazy-feeling body as Huggins fastened the clasp of her beautiful new necklace at the back of her neck so the lovely thing slid into place exactly where Max must have meant it to. She had already been breathless with anticipation when she finally opened the box after looking for a note and not finding one and she certainly hadn't been disappointed.

The necklace inside it was so beautiful it took her breath away. She knew Max had ordered it to be made for her so it wasn't some random purchase he had seen and thought she might like. This was clearly the work of a master jeweller with a clever and exquisitely set trail of gems the same colour as her eyes that had been fashioned into a heart shape made of twined lavender flowers.

When she had finally took her eyes off it and let Huggins put it on for her, the chain turned out to be exactly the right length to slip smoothly into the cleft between her breasts and remind her how much she wanted him to kiss her there until she grew breathless with heady anticipation.

She wore it under her modestly high-cut morning gown and felt the weight of it all the time Huggins fussed with her hair and made sure she was perfectly groomed when she left her maid's expert hands. Max's latest present lay against Georgia's skin in secret, warmed by her body and constantly reminding her of her dream of Max kissing her in so many of her secret places.

She squirmed with frustration as she imagined what could happen, if she was finally brave enough to open that wretched oak door tonight and ask him to kiss her there and there and lower and even lower and truly make love to her for the first time.

'You're up at last, Mama. You do know that it's almost noon, don't you?' Helen said reproachfully when Georgia finally managed to get downstairs with all sorts of distracting fantasies about her husband making love to her in her head. Her senses felt hazy as well as her thoughts and it took far too long for her to snap back into a properly motherly frame of mind and demand to know why her daughters were not in the schoolroom at this time of day.

'Miss Haverstock said we could wait for you down here as long as we were good and didn't make too much mess,' Millie said, although her dubious glance at the scattered papers and books said she wasn't too sure about the last bit either.

'Ah, there you are at last, my dear. Are you ready?' Max said from the doorway with a grin at her bemused state of mind and he should know since he had caused it.

'Uhm, ready for what?' she asked, searching her memory for a clue. The feel of warm gold against her bare skin meant she couldn't think straight. His hungry gaze lingered on the giveaway gold chain where it rested at the base of her neck and even the high ties of the chemise under her round gown couldn't quite hide it. He knew exactly where the pendant was sitting since he must have ordered the pretty gold chain to be this length on purpose.

'Our family picnic, of course, don't you remember?'

'Oh, yes, of course. I forgot that was today,' she lied as she made herself think harder and realised this was the first she had heard of it.

'Scatterbrain,' he teased her and no wonder she glared at him, then tried not to laugh when he winked at her so knowingly it was almost a stage leer.

'You did say only if it was fine, remember?' she improvised.

'So I did and it is. Very fine indeed,' he told her with his gaze on the giveaway strand of fine gold and she wasn't fool enough to think he was talking about the weather.

Helen was obviously getting tired of such puzzling adult conversations, though. 'Max?' she said and held up her arms to be picked up.

'You mustn't,' Georgia said as he bent to oblige her little girl and even Helen wasn't very little any more as a sturdy five-year-old. 'You'll hurt yourself,' she added as both of them stared at her reproachfully.

'No, I'm all healed up and ready, willing and able to hug this beautiful little princess every chance I get. The doctor said so, when he came to look me over for bruises this morning while you were still in bed and even he didn't manage to find any.'

'What about me, then?' Millie demanded with a sulky look at her triumphant little sister perched on Max's arm pretending to be regal.

'You told me when we were discussing the best ways to get to the secret wood you were too big to be carried, so I shall just have to admire you from afar, Princess Amelia. I would be very honoured if you would deign to take my hand, though.'

'Very well,' her elder princess said graciously, then clung to his side as he waited politely for Georgia to walk on ahead of them. She had to blink back a tear of sheer happiness because her daughters had the kind of father figure in their lives she had always dreamt of for them and Max had made it so easy for them to adjust to their new lives.

'Mama has to walk in front of us because she's the queen,' Helen said from her perch and Georgia shook her head sceptically, but kept walking.

She knew Max's gaze was half on her back view and only half on where he was going and she hoped nothing would happen to trip them up. It did feel a little bit queenly, leading her family outside with her husband's eyes appreciative and warm as she swayed her hips self-consciously and tried not to think about doing it in the intimacy of their bedchamber once the girls were fast asleep tonight.

It felt powerful and for the first time in many years the feeling of a man watching her with hungry eyes didn't make her squirm with dread. They had reached the outer courtyard by the time the girls went silent and wide eyed and gazed at the ponies waiting for them in awe.

'Oh, Max, they are perfect,' Georgia gasped and if she hadn't already suspected she was falling in love with him she would have done so when she watched her girls' dearest wish for ponies of their own come true. Why hadn't she thought of it now they lived in the country? Of course they were big enough to have their very own ponies as well as dogs.

'Sam and I had to hunt high and low for exactly the right ones, but at last I think we have found them,' Max said as he set Helen on the smaller pony and Sam solemnly passed her the reins.

'Mine,' she said with absolute contentment and Georgia fought tears again at the sight of her little girl looking so blissfully happy.

'Help me up, Mama,' Millie demanded after greeting her newest friend with almost too much love and the carrot the undergroom held out for her to feed her very own pony.

'Since the mistress is clean, and your shoes ain't, I'd better do that, Miss Amelia,' Sam's deputy said and Millie was too impatient to be on her pony to argue.

'He's wonderful,' Millie said when she was sitting on her own slightly bigger pony. 'What's he called?'

'That's up to you,' Max said.

The girls were still arguing about suitable names for such magnificent creatures when he handed Georgia up into the gig and set his horse to trot down the newly mended north avenue. An avenue whose trees might only be three feet tall, but it was the thought that counted, Max told her as she slewed around to see where her girls were going as they took a path even this neat little carriage was too wide for.

'I'm sure Sam and the lad and Miss Haverstock

will be able to keep them safe between them so stop worrying about them for a while and let them enjoy their first ride together through my fledgling woods, Mrs Chilton,' he said and she turned around and grimaced at her own fussing.

'I know they will be perfectly all right and they need to have their own adventures just as we did as children, but it's my job to worry about them.'

'Mine as well,' he said shortly and she would hurt him if she insisted on being solely responsible for them.

'Ah, but you have just provided them with the biggest treat they have ever had so you're way ahead of me,' she said and settled back into the padded seat as if she was thinking how to outdo him next time. 'It's not fair,' she added childishly for good measure.

'I know, but it's also your job to make sure I don't spoil them.'

'Since you're soft as butter with them I shall have my work cut out,' she said lightly. She wondered how Millie and Helen would feel if he ever had a daughter of his own to spoil and adore as well, but certainly not instead, because Max just wasn't like that.

'I want them to be happy, Georgia, to know for certain they are loved and can feel secure here and are every bit as good as any other child on this planet, not excepting the royal princesses and every male Jascombe ever born. I just wish they were mine instead of his so they would never have had any doubt they are loved and lovable and special to both of us.'

'Spoilt in other words,' she said huskily.

'It's a father's job,' he replied and seemed to be waiting for her to deny him the right to call himself that, but why would she?

'True,' she said, with a pretending-to-be-exasperated sigh. 'Goodness knows what those poor animals will end up being called, though,' she added, hoping he knew she had accepted him as the father of her girls and another fine layer of happiness was growing over her bitter past. She wanted to love Max so completely that surely she would be able to open the door between them soon?

Chapter Fourteen

'I almost understand Timothy, but Slipper?' Max murmured when he was almost certain the girls couldn't hear him because they were chattering so hard to Miss Haverstock about the races they were sure to win on their wonderful new ponies one day.

'Don't ask me,' Georgia said with a shrug and a wry smile for her younger daughter's quirky ways. 'Sometimes she's a mystery to me as well.'

'I suppose we will all get used to it in time and so will he.' How wonderful it would be if the newly christened Slipper was passed on to their next child in line after Helen had outgrown him and Becky's little Phoebe had had her turn if Becky stayed here for that long. Always supposing his patient seduction of his wife ever paid off and they could have more children to hand him on to.

Personally he loved the idea of those children a bit too much and he should probably walk a little further away from his wife if he didn't want the proof of it to become obvious. Yet this time next year they could be walking down this once secret path into the only mature woodland left on his land hand in hand.

He might even have to be very careful to watch where Georgia put her feet on the difficult bits if she was too big with his child to see them for herself. He made himself breathe slowly and steadily and take in every sound and sight of this oddly magical place in order to distract himself from that delightful idea. It was a fantasy he had wanted so much at eighteen and longed for even more dearly now.

'How did the people here keep this place hidden from your predecessor, Max?' Georgia asked and although he hoped she knew he wanted her very much by now, maybe it was as well she didn't know how much that was right now.

He had to exert such iron self-control because he wanted her to know a man didn't have to be a brute when he wanted his wife. He wanted to loosen her fears knot by painfully tight knot so Jascombe's shackles fell away and she could be her true self again.

It was costing him a mighty effort to be this patient, to awaken her needs so his would not come as a terrible shock to her when they finally did at least try to make love fully and completely. Even as an overeager youth Max had sensed she would be a passionate lover if only she loved a man as he had been so desperate for her to love him

Jascombe had tried to kill off that heady potential,

but her shy responses to his careful wooing said the louse had failed. He didn't want to think about Rat Jascombe any more. He wanted to live in the here and now and dream fully grown dreams of Georgia loving him back. He wanted her to feel the joy of it as acutely and deliciously as he did when they finally managed to come together.

He sometimes felt as if he could reach out and touch that Georgia, pull her past the misery of her first marriage into a wondrous here and now, with him, but she needed to feel in control of her own destiny. He wanted her to know she was his equal in every way and never mind what the law said about a husband ruling his wife.

It took so much self-control for him not to push for what he wanted sometimes that he thought he must break and beg for mercy. So far he had managed not to because it would be worth every agonised moment if he had her in his bed being the other half of him, heart and soul one day soon and of her own accord.

Even so, it felt like the right time for him to give that hope another push. He knew she was aware of him as a man and herself as a desirable woman by now, even if she wasn't quite sure what she wanted to do about it yet. He watched her pretending to stroll ahead as if she hadn't a care in the world, but she put up a hand to fiddle with the fine gold chain holding her pendant every now and again, probably without even realising she was doing it.

He suspected the jewel he had made for her kept

reminding her of the sensually aware woman he had always dreamt she could be, if she was loved as he wanted to love her. He had better not fantasise about following that fine gold chain down to the plush valley between her breasts with ardent kisses while their family were around, though. He managed to think of mundane things and even made a sensible reply to her question about the survival of this hidden-away pocket of woodland as he stored that excellent idea away for a more private place and time.

'The valley is so well hidden by the moorland around it I doubt Tolbourne's agents came this far. He never came to Holdfast himself after buying it to strip clean of saleable assets so they had no reason to be very diligent.'

'I'm glad they didn't destroy it. It's so beautiful and feels ancient and I would love to see it again in the spring,' she said dreamily.

Max just made one of the *hmm?* noises he had thought so useful on his way back from wherever they had been one night and, yes, they were useful for hiding his true thoughts. Now he had a new fantasy of her not quite as big with their child by the spring as he daydreamed she might be this time next year, if he was lucky.

Absolute desire ambushed him as he pictured them making sweet love on a bank of spring flowers with nature in full bloom all around them and birds singing them a joyful serenade. *Down, boy*—he had to be tame enough for a family picnic and he wasn't anywhere near that lucky yet. Soon, he promised himself as he caught a glimpse of something almost as dreamy and wanting in her eyes and saw a secretive smile before she turned her head away to keep it to herself. Maybe he could push a little harder to their mutual satisfaction. In private, and much later on when everyone else was safely in bed and the master and mistress of Holdfast would not be disturbed.

'What is it, Huggins?' Georgia murmured sleepily when she heard the outer door of her bedchamber opening very gently.

After an afternoon in the woods with two very over-excited daughters and Max and Leonora and everyone else it took to get a picnic there, she had hoped she would be able to sleep tonight instead of longing for the courage to open the door between her room and Max's. She heard the door close again very softly and hoped her maid had snatched up whatever she had forgotten to take with her and gone away again.

Georgia willed her thoughts back to her happy afternoon with her family and away from the internal door she now knew so well she could probably draw all its knots and crevices from memory. The girls' delight in their new ponies and almost everything about their new lives in a real castle with a real father felt so wonderful she smiled into her pillow and closed her eyes again.

'Good,' she murmured at the thought of them all together in an enchanted-feeling wood. She tried not to even think about getting out of bed to stand by that wretched door tonight and wish it would just melt away without her having to turn the key.

'Hmm?' Max's voice said from far too close for comfort. Was she already dreaming? She cautiously opened her eyes and even by the muted glow of a banked-up fire he was obviously real.

'Max! What the devil are you doing here?' she all but shrieked. She was so shocked by his presence in her bedchamber, when she had been trying not to think about him so near and yet so far away for just one night. He should be on the other side of all that ancient oak and polished iron.

The door had felt such a mighty obstacle on nights when she was wide awake and longing for him and still knew she hadn't got enough bravery in her to unlock the barrier between them. She hardly dared think about those nights now he was actually in here—in her room and not his. He shot her a quizzical look as if she was being obtuse and she knew perfectly well that she wasn't.

'I did knock, but you must have been feeling too sleepy to hear me.'

'Well, I'm certainly not feeling like that now,' she said, sitting bolt upright in bed and staring at him like a mesmerised rabbit at a hungry fox before it broke the spell and ran for its life, yet oddly enough she didn't want to run.

'Excellent, then you might as well take that thing

off while I make up the fire. We wouldn't want you catching cold, now, would we?'

'What?' she said numbly.

All sorts of confused emotions were going around in her head, and very low down in her belly she felt as if she was burning up. There was a sharp need inside her she had never felt even a stir of for any other man but him. Now her heart was racing and her breathing felt so tight that she wanted to put a calming hand over her breastbone, but knew it would give too much away under his amused dark gaze.

'I want you naked and lying on your belly, Georgia, and it will be a lot quicker and less embarrassing if you do it yourself while I turn my back to ensure you will be warm enough.'

'But…' It was no good. She couldn't get anything sensible past suddenly very dry lips, so she just sat and stared at him like a fool.

'I'm following Miss Haverstock's rules,' he told her outrageously.

When had Leonora ruled that a husband could break into his wife's privacy this late at night and make unreasonable demands as if he was merely offering her a cup of tea?

'She is very good at showing your daughters something rather than just telling them about it so they truly take their lessons in,' he explained in the same reasonable voice.

It was beginning to raise her hackles even as she gave a warm shiver at the very sight of him in here.

He had come to her instead of her having to stand wavering on her side of the adjoining door like a coward for one more night and she wasn't quite ready to let him know what an excellent idea it was, not when he was pretending to be so calm and detached.

Her heartbeat was so thunderous in her ears she was almost sure he knew it was racing and was still almost teasing her in a calm and logical manner that would have set her teeth on edge in a less bewildering time and place.

'Don't you dare involve Leonora in this…this invasion,' she managed to protest and thank goodness she had found her voice at last. If he planned to seduce her, she planned to have something to say about it. Even if it was *Hmm, maybe, if you stop being so damned reasonable about it*.

'I didn't think an explanation why I refused to let you massage that devilish stuff into my back after the one time you surprised me was going to persuade you to forgive me. So I am about to show you exactly why I couldn't let you do it again.'

Well, it had hurt her feelings when he made arrangements for his valet to massage his back instead of his wife. She had tried hard not show it, but his absolute refusal to let her touch him again had been painful. Contrary as well, since he had touched her at all sorts of odd times since that earth-shattering kiss and very unsatisfying it was, too.

They were such delicate caresses she had to stifle a gasp and control a shiver of something needy. Then he would walk away as if he was hardly even aware he had touched her and must have had something else on his mind while he was doing it.

'Why couldn't you, then?' she said anyway.

'Ah, no, Georgia, that would be cheating,' he said with a reproachful shake of the head before he turned away from the fire to wash his hands in her wash basin. It felt quite warm in here already. 'And you really do need to take that thing off so I can rub this stuff into your back and *show* you why I couldn't endure you doing it twice for me.'

'I might be willing to take your word for it,' she suggested, but the idea of being naked and maybe a little bit at his mercy did make her feel wickedly curious and she *had* wanted to open that dratted door night after night and now she didn't need to.

'You should never turn down a chance to feel something instead of being told how that something felt to someone else,' he said virtuously. He was drying his hands on her towel as if he was intent on getting every drop of water off, so maybe he was nervous as well as giving her time to make up her mind whether to do as he wanted or play the coward yet again.

That suspicion gave her the courage to raise herself from the mattress and whip her nightgown over her head and off while his back was turned. Thank goodness she had not buttoned it up to the neck tonight. She lay down very quickly on her front, feeling far too much fire-warmed air on her back as shivered with sensual awareness of her husband's gaze on her naked skin.

'You have a beautiful back, Mrs Chilton,' Max told her huskily and from far too close. Her breath was coming in shallow gasps and she told herself it was because this ridiculous position restricted her breasts and never mind if every inch of her could feel his presence even in the places he couldn't see.

'Thank you,' she said between her teeth and heard his warm chuckle as another wave of heady awareness washed over her and she had to keep quiet about it somehow.

'I'm warming this oil with my hands to make sure it doesn't feel cold on your skin,' he explained as the glorious smell of flowers and herbs and high summer wafted towards her averted nose. It smelt headier than the perfume she hadn't yet felt the need to dab on her pulse point this evening to remind her of him kissing her there, thank goodness.

He might realise how needy she was if she had done so and know how often she had longed to feel his kiss there instead of the warm scent of roses and something a lot more complicated. She had hoped to get through one night without the confusion and frustration of missing him as her lover, yet not daring to open that door, and look how that plan was going.

She turned her head to smother a moan into her pillow as his oiled hands met her sensitised skin at last and they were so gentle she wasn't sure if it was a protest or a demand either as he heard it and paused.

She would feel horribly deprived and deflated if he took it as the former and walked away again.

'It smells heavenly,' she murmured and this time she had to smother a sigh of relief in her pillow as he took it as the encouragement it was meant to be and carried on smoothing the fragrant stuff into her sensitised skin. It felt like bliss as he massaged her tensed muscles and she wanted to stop thinking altogether and simply feel and lie here silently wanting him.

'It certainly smells a lot better than liniment,' he said with a smile in his voice she should not know about when her eyes were closed and her face was averted. Then he spread his long-fingered hands across both her shoulders at the same time and she had never realised how delicious it would feel to have his work-roughened hands so sensitive and praising on that neglected part of her. Who would have thought a back could feel so receptive to a man's touch? No, not any man, only him.

'It was meant to do you good,' she murmured past the urge to just lie here and moan at the feel of her muscles relaxing under his hypnotic touch, even if the rest of her wanted to tense as tightly as the skin of a drum and question if she really wanted more intimacy and an even more lover-like intent from him.

'Does this feel as if it's doing you good?' he murmured in her nearest ear. At least he was tall enough not to have to straddle her as she had him because she wasn't sure she could lie helpless under a man like that, even if it was him.

'I'm not sure yet,' she murmured and it was true.

His touch on her achingly aware body made her feel such a sweet, hot sense of anticipation that she wanted to shift and writhe against the sheet to try to soothe it or did she just want to feed it? She wasn't quite sure she wanted what might come next if she did let her true feelings out and he responded. He would know she wanted him to do something about this sweet hot ache at the heart of her if she moaned with delight and gasped a demand for more.

'Maybe you should keep doing it so I can find out,' she added with a shiver of expectation he was hardly going to take for cold when every inch of her felt as if it was blushing.

'Hmm,' he said in rather a tight-sounding voice and for a moment she forgot to be puzzled and aroused at the same time as the feel of her tense muscles loosening under his deeper touch took away tensions she hadn't even known she had.

She felt him shift and kneel on the bed at her side as he worked his way lower and his thumbs ran either side of her spine to work on the back of her waist, whatever that was called and she didn't care right now. Until now she could fool herself that his touch was therapeutic, meant to soothe the kinks and twists out of her muscles and even help her to sleep—as if that was even possible with such heat and curiosity and excitement as he was building so skilfully inside her.

It was urging her to fight the fears she still couldn't quite banish, telling her it would be worth the effort. The fire inside her felt as sharp and hot as slow-burning lightning. She had to bite the pillow to stop herself gasping a frantic plea for more that she didn't understand wanting. He caressed the indentation of her waist on both sides from his position half crouching over her and she frowned with concern for his newly healed back and shifted closer to the edge of the mattress so he wouldn't have to twist it to reach her.

There was so much tenderness under the fire and she had longed for him every night as she stood in front of that stupid door and hated the fact she was too afraid to reach out and turn the key. There was fear on both sides, she realised now. He was afraid of hurting her, reminding her of past terror, of Edgar's sick tyranny. She felt it in Max's gentle touch, heard it in his shallow breathing as if he was still trying to clamp down on whatever hot urgency a man felt for his lover.

She did want to find out how that felt, didn't she? They had always had a different life together, another language instead of the… No, she wasn't going to think of her life with another man; it would be an insult to who they were now. She gasped as Max's soothing hands reached her bare backside. How could she hide her secret desperation any longer when it felt so all-consuming that everything except him, in here with her, slid clean out of her mind?

She moaned out loud this time as his massaging hands ran along her hips and she raised them from the bed as her body took charge. She was so glad that it had when she heard him growl something needy and frustrated. She hadn't known she wanted him to get to the core of this heady longing and show her how true satisfaction felt for the first time so badly, but she did now.

She couldn't hide her frantic need for more from him a moment longer. She put weight on to her shaking arms and pushed upwards, even as Max's hands praised her curvaceous derrière and she heard his ragged sigh. She could almost feel him trying to tighten the reins on his own fierce need and she really didn't want him to. At last he had coaxed her to find enough courage, to want him beyond reason.

Whatever it cost her, she was willing to pay it with him. Yet when she tried to force the words to tell him so between her lips they wouldn't come. Never mind her last shred of modesty—she had to face him now. She needed to show him what she wanted now that language had deserted her.

She twisted to face him with all the heat and hurry her inner woman wanted from him in her eyes and she just had to hope he would read them rightly. He looked almost as overheated as she was, but as if he thought he should tear himself away and go back to his own chilly bedchamber—when she had all this sweet desperation dammed up inside her so desperate for an outlet.

She shook her head, pushed up on to hands and knees and faced him naked as the day she was born. She made a clumsy attempt at undoing his cravat when he still didn't seem to take her naked invitation to stay and show her what she had been missing. She even tried to pull his shirt out of his breeches.

Her fingers didn't seem to be working any better than her tongue and thank goodness he must have taken his coat and waistcoat off before he came in here to tempt and maybe even seduce his own wife.

'I wanted you so much that day I was on fire for hours after you left my room,' he told her huskily. 'But are you certain you want me to stay here now?' he asked so unsteadily she almost wanted to cry.

'Yes.' She managed a word at last and nodded for good measure, so he was sure he hadn't misunderstood her.

She recalled that day and the feel of his mighty muscles under her probing fingers as she had tried to fight shyness and a wicked twist of desire for his manly body deep down inside her, even as she told herself she was only trying her best to do exactly what the doctor had told her to.

'I— Oh, I can't talk,' she told him with acute frustration.

'It doesn't matter…don't try,' he whispered and fumbled his shirt from his breeches.

She could hardly wait to get her hands on his

body. She was so fascinated by the shape of hard muscles across his tight belly. The dusting of fine dark hairs across his broad chest intrigued her, too. She wanted to explore him with all her senses and that surprised her, but as he was half-naked now maybe she should remember to be scared instead.

'Just feel, Georgia. This is me, Max. You can feel how you and I are together,' he whispered as if he knew what she was thinking. Then he gently pulled her closer so their bodies could do just that and it felt so wonderful she forgot to be afraid.

Max would wait however long it took her to adjust to this shivery strangeness. She wanted him so close and even closer, of course she did, but he was a potent and fully adult male nowadays. He was also shaking with the urgency of wanting her, holding back as if he would still fight his need into a corner and go if this was as far as she could manage to get them tonight.

Instead of the last traces of fear she knew he was dreading, a huge new need swept right through her as she felt his sigh, felt it on her sensitised skin at the same time as she heard it leave his mouth. Desire was like a force of nature within her and almost beyond her control. It was so strong she only wanted to feel and taste and know every inch of his salty, intriguing skin. Her world had narrowed to just them, just him.

Chapter Fifteen

'Max,' Georgia whispered wonderingly and it was all she needed to say for him to understand her perfectly as he smiled down into her eyes. They both finally knew this would be their wedding night and never mind all the others between their marriage and now; it would be worth waiting for.

'Georgia,' he breathed her name as their bodies kissed together again and the sweetest shocks swept through her at the contact of his skin against hers. It felt like that to her, as if their whole bodies were kissing and singing with exquisite sensations and how heady it felt to know it was the same ones running through both of them and it felt like acute desire to her. Never mind what came next, for a long and precious moment of recognition and acceptance it didn't matter as they looked into each other's eyes and just felt the heat and promise of skin on skin, lover against lover. Georgia and Max.

'Show me,' she murmured as she got some words back and realised she was wrong. It did matter, because she wanted even more than sensation, she wanted everything. 'Show me who we are now, Max, who we can be together,' she managed to get out before he kissed her deeply and so hungrily, as if he couldn't hold himself back a moment longer and he must have been hungry for this for so very long.

It felt as if a mighty river had been dammed as the barriers holding him back broke even as he tried his hardest to shore them up again. She wanted them to fall, wanted him to be totally himself with her for the first time in far too long. She felt so reckless and powerful as she kissed him back and explored the back of his neck with eager fingers.

There was such tension there and in his broad shoulders as she learnt him all over again by touch. He was so familiar yet so very different from her. He was her man, her lover, as if they had been newly made. Max's kiss was long and deep this time and he wanted her so much she felt his hands shake again.

It took her last trace of fear away because it let her know he was vulnerable, too. Her exploring hands reached his narrow waist and she pouted into his hungry mouth to say his breeches were still in place, even if he had shrugged his braces off to remove his shirt, *and* they were still fastened.

'I could frighten you,' he warned her unsteadily.

'No, you couldn't, not you,' she argued and it was true. This wasn't bravery, it was simply how they were always meant to be as fully adult lovers. She could be furious with herself for not knowing that at eighteen later, when she wasn't so busy loving him.

'I need you a lot,' he said between clenched teeth as she fumbled with his buttons and who would have thought she would be the overeager one of the two of them when they finally got around to making love to one another? 'And I will need you a lot sooner than I should if you don't stop doing that right now.'

'You always have to make the rules, don't you?' she argued grumpily and felt his chuckle just before a long moan shook through him instead as she ran her hands under the waistband of his breeches to get to his narrow flanks and encourage him to take the dratted things off so they could be as exposed as one another, equally vulnerable and equally strong.

'As if you have ever obeyed any of the ones I made up even when we were children,' he still managed to say shakily, but he did unfasten his breeches at last so that was something.

'I'm certainly not going to start now,' she told him and they were familiar and dear to one another as ever with the added bonus of acute, edgy and achingly hot desire. He was the other side of her, her other half and a lovely, loving and sensuous side it was, too.

'Only one rule, my Georgia; I will always stop if you don't want to go on,' he said so seriously she had to forget Edgar for Max's sake as well as her own when they got to what came next.

'If I ever want you to stop, I know you will, but it won't be tonight,' she whispered into his nearest ear and experimented with her feminine power again by running an appreciative hand over his very tense, tight buttocks and his long moan of desire and even tighter-feeling muscles said his need of her had just got even mightier than it was before.

'You're enjoying this, aren't you?' he almost accused her as his rigidly aroused male member went even more rigid and she hadn't thought that was even possible.

She wanted him so much it was like a hot pool of pure joy and heat and longing inside her. Knowing she could do that to him and he would still hold back until he thought she was ready felt so tender and loving she hardly dared think about it any more deeply in case she really did cry. That would be that for him, unless she could manage to persuade him they were happy tears, and it wasn't worth the risk.

She plastered herself against his long and eager-for-her body until there wasn't even room for that provocative silk scarf he had given her between them. She stretched lazily against him, revelling in the feel of his slightly hair-roughened skin against her hungrily aroused nipples even if she had to stretch her body against his to get them there.

She heard his breath go shallow and light as she let her hands wander down his spine and she let out a moan of hunger herself as her breathing went faster and her knees wobbled until they were next door to useless.

'Every moment,' she admitted in his ear and enjoyed the stretch and lithe effort of getting even closer to all of him.

She knew she was pushing him too far for fairness, but it felt so wonderful to know he would still fight his need and all the stormy desire in his eyes when she finally met them.

'Did you just grind your teeth?' she asked him and tried to hide a smile of witchy satisfaction by kissing him slowly and deeply and with their tongues telling tales about all the things their bodies were about to do together and she still wasn't afraid of him.

'Whatever it takes,' he told her gruffly.

'Then undo us, Max,' she said huskily. 'Free us both,' she added with a long, sweet shudder of awareness and lowered her exploring hand to his straining sex, but he got there first and stopped her with his breath stalled and a protesting groan.

'Touch me there and all I'll be able to do is fall apart in front of you. That's not how our first loving should be,' he told her seriously. She stopped because he must know the limits of his own self-control and she didn't want to spend another night on the wrong side of his bedchamber door, wanting him with every inch of her being, but not being able to push past that woody old barrier to make love with him.

'Get on with it then, you sluggard,' she ordered and had to chuckle at his look of offended male pride when his straining sex proved he wanted to be anything but slow.

'Witch,' he accused her and toppled them backwards on to the bed so he was lying flat on his back and she was splayed against him, looking down into his darkest of dark brown eyes as they told her all sorts of stories about how desperately he wanted her.

'Like this?' she said and had to look closer, see his face under hers in such fine detail, feel his breath on her open mouth, slick hers and then his with her tongue. She wanted him so much that words were leaving her again and actions spoke louder than them anyway.

'Yes, take me, Mrs Chilton, I'm all yours,' he said and she hardly heard the words for the powerful feel of them forming so close to her mouth it felt as if they echoed right through her receptive body.

'You can't just lie there and leave me to do all the work,' she managed to protest.

'A joint effort, then,' he promised and kissed her so deeply she forgot all about who was where.

When his urging hands raised her just enough to take him inside her, she splayed her legs and did exactly that without even a hitch in her great need to have him there, finally, completing them as lovers after far too many years apart. It didn't feel like an invasion at all. It felt like such an exquisite pleasure that she nearly melted all over him before they could explore this astonishing intimacy even an iota further.

'Not yet,' he told her and took over enough of their ride to steady the pace and show her there was some very fine scenery along the way.

It was such a lovely rhythm she took it up with a moan of intense delight. She hadn't even known this world of heat and light and intimacy existed until tonight and it felt so right that she had found it with him. Max rose under her as she came down on his mighty shaft and he filled her so deliciously again that she shook with tenderness, even as such an avid fire burned inside her that she gasped with indescribable need.

The driving desire for more and more made her rise further and faster in time with him and it felt as if they were sending each other frantic as they reached for another lovely place she had never known about before him. She heard words she hadn't known she had shouted into the friendly gloom and felt his rich chuckle at the frantic demands she was making of him both inside and outside her body.

The lovely, urgent connection of him inside her made him feel a part of her in every way and a very fine part he was, too. She still spared a moment to be glad this area of the castle had very thick walls and sturdy old oak doors to keep the sound of the mistress of the house in extremis inside her chamber with the master of it, where they belonged.

Max bucked under her, as if he was having trouble holding back his frantic need to get to a mysterious destination she sensed so close now they could almost touch but not quite reach. He suckled on one of her achingly aroused nipples and she keened a wild, demanding moan because words had gone again as the hottest, sweetest urgency made her shake with wonder.

He was her lover and such a tender, strong, passionate one there wasn't an ounce of fear left in her, anywhere. She wondered if a woman could expire from sheer sensual delight and their very joint effort. This total intimacy felt like such a glorious surprise. Surging even higher inside her, Max added to the blaze and suddenly there was nothing gentle about their heat and urgency and she didn't want there to be. His mouth was hot on hers, his hands guiding, shaping, praising her and his very urgent sex was frantic inside her.

She bucked in unison with him as their whole bodies became desperate. She felt as if she was racing out of control as an even greater force was striving to be felt inside her, with him. Then it span up into heaven knew where and she felt Max's longer, deeper thrusts as if he was desperate to get them up to an even giddier height and he let out a mighty roar of extreme satisfaction as they found it at last. They got there together and her moans matched his deeper ones and it was the sweetest music she had ever heard.

She convulsed on his sex as he drove up into her and it felt glorious. Mysterious and wondrous and absolute bliss as she bowed backwards in absolute pleasure and heard and felt and just knew he was with her every inch of the way. It was such complete togetherness, so intimate she no longer knew where she started and he began.

They were so sweetly entangled, so lost in ecstasy she felt her eyes roll back in her head as pure bliss spread out all around them in a new land, made from their complete pleasure in one another. She felt Max find his release at last and her most joyous convulsions yet wrapped him so deep inside her it felt as if they were flying together.

They held on to one another for comfort and long, sweet joy as she tightened her sex on his one last time and finally sank down, breathless and boneless, on his mighty prone body and sobbed with so many dazzling emotions and feelings she had no idea how to untangle them and tell him how remade she felt after her first ever lovemaking.

'Ah, don't cry, my love,' he whispered as he felt her tears and her head felt so heavy as she sank on to his still heaving torso there was nowhere to hide them from him.

She felt his hand shaking as he smoothed her very disordered curls and anxiety seemed to come off him in waves even as he wound one of her dishevelled locks around his finger as if he couldn't get enough of the feel of her completely undone against his mighty body like this. It felt like far too much effort to move off him and lie sated and a little bit worn out by his side instead of on top of his powerful and still heaving chest.

'Please don't cry,' he added as if every one of her tears was hurting him and she felt his great sigh of protest through her own body.

'I can't help it, I'm so happy,' she told him with a sniffle and an unbecoming snort of laughter, 'and neither of us has a stitch on so I can't ask you for your handkerchief.' She sobered and stared down at him with wonder. 'I just didn't know, Max, I didn't know we could feel like this, be like this, become so very much more together than we are apart.'

'And now you do know it, will you unlock that wretched door between our rooms at last?' he asked her gruffly and she knew he was trying to disguise his joy that she obviously didn't regret a single moment of what they had just done together.

She had to unlock a lot more than the door between them, though, didn't she? She needed to unlock her true self as well. Somehow she would have to admit everything she was and was not eight years ago, before they could love freely and for good as husband and wife.

Never mind the absolute joy and pleasure he had just shown her, she had to be honest with him for both their sakes. She had to prove this was more than the most beautiful physical pleasure a woman could ever feel with her one and only real lover. Show he was more to her than the finest lover a woman could long for in her wildest dreams and some of them had been very wild indeed, about him, but not a single one of them had lived up to the reality of loving Max.

'Yes, Husband, I will,' she promised him with a sleepy smile into his chest that she hoped he knew about by feel alone and sighed a very contented sigh, then she yawned and went to sleep with Max's heart-beat steady in her ear and his arms holding her close and oh, so safe.

Chapter Sixteen

'I have asked Leonora and Becky if they mind being left in charge of the girls for a day or two while we visit our parents,' Georgia informed Max the following morning.

As they had only just begun on the most delightful part of keeping their marriage vows he thought she might have consulted him first. He didn't want to stay at Flaxonby or Riverdale tonight or the next one and especially not the one after that. He wanted to spend each one here, loving his wife to the edge of reason, again and again for preference, in one of their beds, under their own roof and with a very solid old oak door between them and the rest of the world so they could make as much noise as they liked.

Staying with her parents at Riverdale or at empty, echoing Flaxonby, even when Zach and Martha were elsewhere, would not provide them with as much stone and oak ensured privacy as Holdfast could.

'Why?' he asked and felt his heart stop dancing and start sinking again as he recognised her closed expression and realised she wasn't going to tell him until they got there and maybe not even then.

He thought last night proved they had something special and spectacular and worth lingering over between them. Growing it into complete love and trust as husband and wife one day would be his favourite project ever and the sooner she knew this was unique and worth fighting for every moment of every day, the better.

He watched her holding something of herself in reserve with him and it felt as if Jascombe was standing between them once again, like a lingering poison that had never quite left her system. He could almost hear the man's evil little snicker as his ghost whispered he was Georgiana's husband first and he had taught her not to give that much of herself to any man.

'Because I need to see my parents and your mother writes that she is feeling lonely now Zachary and Martha are at Greygil yet again and Becky is living here with us.'

'I suspect that is partly because she wanted to fuss over Martha more than Martha wants to be fussed over. My sister-in-law has insisted she and Zachary are needed at Greygil for the autumn gathering of the flocks. No doubt once they are there they will decide to stay until the baby is born. Are you sure you want to face my mother's speculative looks and not very subtle hints that even more grandchildren would be very welcome?' he challenged his wife's plans, partly because he felt he should warn her what to expect and partly because he wanted her to change her mind and stay here with him.

He didn't want Georgia to forget they might have added one more grandchild to his mother's tally last night and again this morning. He intended to try again tonight and tomorrow night and for as many nights as she felt able to until they got there, even if they had to keep a lot quieter about it if everyone at Flaxonby or Riverdale were not to be fully aware they were working very hard on making a bigger family for Holdfast to echo with as soon as humanly possible.

There was no better way to make their marriage real for Georgia and so very unlike her last one than a dedicated quest for them to have children together, God willing. He couldn't wait to show her how much he loved feeling and seeing his baby growing inside her, if they were blessed with one after all those hearty endeavours.

It would never be about heirs or heiresses for him, but the sheer wonder of a new and unique little being half from each of them. Yet Georgia seemed determined to tear them away from their marriage bed before its sheets were properly cold. If he thought too hard about his heady fantasy of her big with his child, he would try to coax her back upstairs to try again to make one with him and it clearly wasn't what she wanted in the full light of day.

'I expect you are right,' she said.

Was he? He had to search past his frustration and worry to remember what he was supposed to be right about. Ah, yes, his mother dropping blatantly tactless hints about wanting more grandchildren. What a very sensible woman the Dowager Lady Elderwood was and if his wife wanted to hear them at first hand he certainly wasn't going to stop his mother making less than gentle enquiries about when they might expect to welcome their first child together.

'At least your mama will try to be subtle about it—I'm not so sure about my own,' Georgia said with a rosy flush to say she was looking back on last night as well and wondering if they were already due to be parents in nine months' time.

Now, wouldn't that be wonderful? Her blush and that oddly shy look away from his hot gaze said she thought so, too. She hadn't had any reason to do that until today and at least it was a reminder of how far they had come together. He just thought they had come further than they apparently had when he woke up with her in his arms early this morning and whispered why couldn't they do it all again before she rang for Huggins to help her dress?

She had blushed as she twisted round to watch him with speculative, inviting eyes so they did just that and he had only just turned that infernal key in the locked door between their rooms and gone back to his own room when Huggins's tap on the door said her mistress was being a slug-abed today and wasn't it about time she was up and doing?

They had even met at the breakfast table with a hard and hasty kiss before the head footman came in with fresh toasted muffins and caught them at it. Georgia had blushed deliciously and Max thought they were embarking on their first proper day as man and wife together here, He intended to remember every second of it for future nostalgia and many repeats of his matchless joy and contentment because his wife was now his lover as well.

After she had lain in his arms when their early morning interlude was over, while he revelled in the lovely feel of her nestling her spent body against his as she dreamt of goodness knew what and her breathing steadied in time with his, she must have been planning this journey. It felt as if she was standing back from them as lovers again, refusing to be all in all to him as he wanted to be for her.

He couldn't read her thoughts now, had no idea how she really felt about him as they stood watching one another and his confidence in who they were now as man and wife was in danger of seeping away.

'I shall ride,' he said abruptly and saw a flicker of hurt in her eyes before she veiled it from him. So, here they were again—dancing around one another like performers in a stately minuet and of course he must ride to avoid the disappointment of knowing she was hiding from him again even after those two won-drous conflagrations in Mrs Chilton's bedchamber.

'Very well, I will meet you at Riverdale,' she said as if it took a lot more resolution to play the stiffly formal Mrs Chilton than he wanted to know about.

He could take it back, climb into her elegantly comfortable travelling carriage with her and…

No, don't think about the and *part of that idea, Chilton, it will unman you.*

Georgia probably needed a nap rather than yet more husbandly demands now they had got started on being lovers. Even if she didn't want to sleep, he could hardly oust her maid from the seat opposite and pull up the blinds so they could make love yet again as the miles flashed past and all the servants would know exactly what the master and mistress of Holdfast were doing behind them.

She must have been planning this trip ever since Max went back to his own room to bathe and shave and try to stop humming joyful tunes under his breath only a couple of hours ago. Or was she doing it as she lay in his arms this morning with that dreamy smile on her lovely face and he thought it was solely meant for him?

Never mind the prickle of unease, the vague sense of being hard done by that twisted last night and this morning into something less than he had been so sure it was at the time—he had to change into riding gear and get ready to escort his lady back to their old homes in Yorkshire and whatever she wanted to do there more than make love to him as often as such a delayed honeymoon might have excused them doing.

Georgia was gone by the time he and Sam met in the stable yard so they could ride cross country to catch up with her neat travelling carriage and four. Her sudden need to get away from Holdfast, the place where they had finally become husband and wife last night, felt dangerous to his most cherished hopes and dreams. He should be feeling overjoyed to have made love to the woman he had always dreamed of loving, but doubt whispered she might be regretting it in the cold light of day. Maybe this sudden journey was meant to set him at a distance again and he wasn't sure he could stop there this time.

Now they were here. As Max had only caught up with the carriage just before they reached River-dale Village, that felt tardy and a little bit insulting of him. Georgia wanted to get this over with before she lost her nerve. So much of her was arguing she was stupid to have done this. That she should have stayed at Holdfast and waited to find the right words to say what she needed to say to Max. It wasn't as if they didn't know one another through and through and a lot better than they had done even yesterday.

But she had tried so hard to find the words to tell him how she felt about him as she lay dreamy and sated in his arms this morning and they just would not come. Not even while he was still there with her, still holding her as if he loved the feel of them naked and so close together.

She had been so sure that words didn't matter while he still held her, but as soon as he went back to his room and Huggins bustled in, her inability to tell her own husband that she loved him felt choking and almost terrible. She wanted him to know, wanted to tell him she loved him beyond her wildest dreams of loving. She needed to tell him she had been such a fool when they were both young she almost hated the younger version of herself for being so stupid.

That silly headlong version of her hadn't even seen his young love for her when it was so tender and unprotected she must have hurt him so very badly. It felt as if she had hurt that boy so much, how could the man he was now ever truly forget her insensitivity and love her as he might have done back then?

Now she knew she had to dig the words out of herself and give him everything she had refused to give him in the past. She could only start from here somehow, where all that denial and stupidity had begun when they were eighteen and still living on their family estates. It was all she could offer him and hope to convince him he had been right all along— they *were* born to love each other and she had been such a fool not to see it, too.

She was as tense as a bow string now and even that felt wrong after the lovely relaxation she had revelled in just a few hours ago in Max's arms as they made love by daylight and it was even more powerful and deliciously wonderful than it had been last night. He had made her feel so much, got her to see herself as he saw her for a magical few hours. She had felt truly beautiful and he had given her such a heady sense of freedom that she marvelled that marriage to him had seemed like a trap when they began it.

She had wasted six whole weeks in ignorance of what truly loving her husband felt like, but now she knew she had to do this to let him know she really did love him. It felt as if she wouldn't be able to find the right words to say how she felt about him unless she made things clear to both her parents at long last. She just hoped Max would still want her afterwards.

'Oh, what a lovely surprise,' her mother cried as her daughter entered the room with Max looming behind her. No doubt he was wondering as much as her mother and father why he hadn't even been given time to go upstairs and change out of his riding clothes.

'Good afternoon, Mama,' Georgia said with a quick kiss on the cheek for her still very handsome mother while her stern glance dared Mrs Welland to comment on the aroma of horse as she shook hands with her son-in-law with such pursed lips they said it for her.

'I have sent for Papa,' Georgia added concisely. Then she stood silently waiting for him because this wasn't a social call and she was too tense to sit opposite her mother like a meek little daughter and take tea. 'And before you say or even imply anything about his manners, I asked Max not to take the time to go to Flaxonby so he can bathe and change after riding here so hastily at my request.'

'I can't imagine why you didn't travel in the carriage with my daughter, Maxwell,' her mother said anyway and Georgia sighed impatiently.

'I don't suppose you can, Mrs Welland,' Max said blandly.

Despite her growing tension Georgia almost laughed as she imagined what he was thinking and why he chose to ride rather than scandalise the coachman and groom and where on earth would they have put Huggins?

'Ah, Perkins didn't imagine you, then, my love,' her father said as he entered the room.

He kissed his daughter on both cheeks and gave her his usual bear hug before greeting Max easily and Georgia felt a little more sure that this had been the right thing to do. Not only did she need to free herself and tell Max how she felt about him, but she thought her father deserved better than her mother had been willing to allow him until now.

'There is something I should have told you both a long time ago,' she said and in the tense silence as she searched for the right words she could almost feel her father and husband silently arguing with her, but her mother needed to know and Georgia needed to say it. 'You always wanted me to marry a nobleman, Mama. You trained me up to do so, taught me to flatter or condescend depending on the rank of those above and below the lofty place in society you expected me to fill one day.'

'I taught you manners, taste and refinement. A lady needs the esteem of those around her and there's nothing wrong with respecting rank as it deserves.'

'Not as it deserves maybe, but in my experience that's not very much. Rank is just a reward for a deed done by a man's ancestors, good or bad. It says nothing about him as a person.'

'Nonsense, proper respect for rank is the bedrock of society.'

'Then I pity us all, Mama, because Edgar hit me for the first time the morning after our wedding and he went on doing it whenever I wasn't with child until the day he died. His father's rank and generations of privilege made sure he had sturdy enough doors to hide it behind and enough influence to keep the rumours he was a beast and a bully at bay. The sad truth is Lord Edgar Jascombe was no better than the tavern bully who gives his wife a black eye when he gets home drunk simply because she exists and he likes doing it.'

'No! No, I won't believe it. He was the son of a duke; he could not have been so cruel to his own wife.'

'Oh, but he was, Mama. I hid the truth from you because I thought it would break your heart to know your precious son-in-law had feet of clay. I hid the bruises and the yanked muscles and all the humiliations he liked heaping on me from everyone except Max. Even after Edgar died and I was so ashamed he had made a victim of me for so long I went on protecting you from what I had been subjected to by one of your precious lords.'

There was a long silence and she remembered the pretty room her mother had decorated for her with so much love when she was a girl and knew her mother loved her despite her ridiculous ambitions for her only child. This must be hurting her, but protecting her from the truth wasn't doing any good either.

Learning to hide her feelings, to be silent and hold back the truth, had to be the reason why her tongue tied itself in knots whenever she tried to tell Max she loved him. The words stuck in her throat even now and she knew she had to unlock them somehow, but what if it was too late and Max didn't believe her?

'I… I don't know what to say,' her mother said as love for her daughter fought with her long-held belief that peers of the realm were the human equivalent of Greek gods come down from Olympus to walk the earth with mere mortals.

'I had to get you to see what you are throwing away, Mama. I didn't mean to make you cry, only to finally get you to understand how lucky you are to have married a good man. Papa is a good and faithful husband and he's kind, but you have set him lower than any so-called gently born male simply because his father made a fortune in trade. No, don't stop me from telling Mama the truth she should already know about you, Papa. You *are* a good man and I know to my cost how hard they are to find.'

She paused as the most crucial words of all threatened to seize in her throat again, but she had to force them out this time.

'Max is one, but I turned my back on him because I wanted a title and to live in a stately pile when I was eighteen, because you brought me up to think that would be so wonderful how could I not want it, Mama. Max loved me when we were both eighteen, but I ignored his love, made light of it and hurt him so badly that I don't know if I can ever forgive myself for what I did to him back then.

'He was the only person I could turn to when Edgar died and I had to tell someone how awful my life with him had been. Max married me to save me from having to live at Mynham again with the girls, in the same miserable rooms where I was beaten and humiliated for three long years by my first and supposed-to-be noble husband.'

'Max is…' She paused again as she searched for the right words and he went to speak, but she put a finger on his lips to ask him not to. This wasn't the time or place to be so aware of his mouth under her touch and want to caress it, then stare into his dark eyes with all she felt for him in her own. 'Max is going to let me speak,' she said with a severe look, 'because he loves me.'

'Ah, very well,' he said with a nod to say that *was* why and he was glad she knew it.

'Max has been my best friend since we were old enough to get into mischief together, but I still broke his heart when we were young. I hate the thought of the ruthless little title hunter I was back then. I had a second son with a better title than his and a suite of grand rooms in a grand house in my sights and I wasn't going to be diverted by a silly little thing like love.'

'If Lord Chert did not marry or produce a son, you could have been a duchess one day,' her mother said as if she was still clinging on to that foolish old dream.

'A duchess chained to a monster. Why can't you see love is far more important than rank and privilege even now, Mama? I have more real love and joy in my life than the Duke of Ness and his stuffy peers have between them now because I love Max and I think he still loves me. I love my husband and you can't imagine how sweet it is for me to be able to say how much I love Max when I hated my first husband so bitterly I was glad he died and set me free even if I did feel guilty about it.'

At last she could say it and now she had started she couldn't seem to stop.

'You love me?' Max said so quietly Georgia had to step closer to hear him and almost forgot they had an audience.

'I do,' she said on a long sigh as the ache in her throat finally melted away.

'And about bloody time, too,' he said and she put

her hand over his mouth in shock at his language and in a lady's drawing room, too! Suddenly she could laugh as well as tell him she loved him and it felt absolutely wonderful.

He was her darling Max, her everyday sort of husband as well as the man who put the stars in the sky for her and made that everyday world seem so much brighter. Her life was real with him, this extraordinary man who had loved her even when she didn't deserve it. She loved him so much it made silly young Georgia look more of a fool than ever.

She smiled up at him like a besotted fool, grabbed his hand and turned so they could face her parents together. 'I had to try to make you see what you are throwing away, Mama. The character of a man is all that matters, you see? Not what his ancestors did to be made into lords or dukes—and that's usually best not enquired into too deeply.'

Chapter Seventeen

'Do you think knowing the truth about your splendid first marriage will change your mother in any way?' Max asked Georgia as if he didn't think it could.

'I don't know,' she said. 'I can only hope my father will finally be forgiven by his own wife for not being born into the purple.'

'Why did you feel you needed to say all that to me in front of them? Why not just tell me, Georgia?' Max asked a bit too seriously for comfort.

'We would never have got half a mile along the road here if I said it to you first, now, would we?'

'And why would that have been so wrong?'

'If you must know, I didn't have either the courage or the words to say it to you until we got here, where it all began when we were children and then suddenly we weren't. I was such a fool to turn my back on the idea of you when I thought I was a woman at eighteen and I was just taller and more of an idiot.

'How could I have been so *stupid*, Max? Why did I not see you when you had obviously seen me? Because you didn't have a title and my mother said it was a basic requirement for the man I would marry, I suppose,' she said, answering her own question. 'Papa would have given his permission for us to wed if only I had wanted to marry you back then and never mind what Mama said, so I can't even blame it all on her. I have to hate my young self for causing you so much pain for such a very unworthy cause, Max.'

'It wasn't that bad,' he said with a shrug to minimise her stupidity all those years ago and she knew she had to own up to it if they were going to have an honest marriage.

'I know otherwise, I know how much you suffered,' she said shortly. The carriage had stopped in front of grand neo-classical Flaxonby Hall, but she signalled the startled footmen to keep away.

'How?'

'Becky told me that, too.'

'I'll strangle her, slowly.'

'You will have to get past me first. She was right to tell me how much you hurt and how hard you fought to forget me once I was married to Edgar. I thought you had forgotten me in those studies at Cambridge that everyone seemed to think you were enjoying so much.

'I used to wish I was a man so I could join you during that first year while I waited for Millie to be born and hated every part of my splendid new life as a breeding mare for the ducal succession and chattel to my supposedly noble husband. After she was born I loved my baby too much to wish myself anything other than her mother, but I envied you so bitterly until then and all the time you were miserable and trying so hard to forget me.'

'I did try very hard to do so, Georgia,' he said with the bitterness of it in his eyes as he recalled the passionate, hurt boy who wrote out his resolutions to forget her over and over again. 'You were my best friend as well as the girl I thought would be the love of my life, so I was lonely as well as furious and so frustrated without you.'

'I doubt you were frustrated for very long,' she said and thought of the eager mistress she had invented for him at the beginning of the summer and felt jealous all over again.

'Oh, you are flattering me, my love. I was a spotty and not very rich youth at the time.'

'I'm so sorry you were lonely,' she lied and didn't want to think of the boy he was then sleeping in the arms of an eager lover, or the man he became later doing it either. If that made her a bad woman then so be it. '*I* want you and you're not in the least bit spotty now.'

This was meant to be her grand gesture, a semi-public declaration of all he meant to her, since she couldn't find the words or courage to say it to him in private. It looked the very opposite of grand as they sat in a motionless carriage outside his brother's fine but empty house.

'I might be a weedy man of nearly seven and twenty at this very moment if you had realised what a fine man I was back then, my love. It was missing you so hopelessly that made me study hard for my degree to distract myself from loving you and I am rather proud of it. You are the real reason I took on Holdfast when my brother and Martha offered it to me as well, because I needed to work hard to forget you and it really did need me.

'I certainly would not have become the splendid specimen of manhood before you if it wasn't for you. I would probably have sat back and been Zach's idle little brother for the rest of my life, not fitted for army, navy or the church and not much use to anyone. You are the one who put steel in my backbone and made me the man I am today.'

She could see he really believed it, but she thought he would have become more than he was born to be anyway, because he had such energy and verve that something else would have touched his heart enough to make him fight for it if she wasn't such an idiot at eighteen. There was no point in her telling him so, though. If he wanted to think she was responsible for the fine man he had made himself into, she was quite happy for him to carry on with that particular delusion.

'I do good work, even by accident,' she told him

with a besotted smile and an appreciative feel of his nearest wide shoulder to admire it more closely.

'You are the lodestone of my life, Georgia, plain and simple. I simply love you and I think I always have, even when I was trying to convince myself otherwise. I know I always will now you are my wife and finally have the good sense to love me back.'

'Thank you,' she breathed between rather wobbly lips and saw a protest in his dark eyes. 'I mean, thank you for keeping on doing it, despite all the reasons I gave you not to.'

'Like being married to somebody else, then being a hurt and damaged widow even I wasn't brash enough to try to woo for five long years?'

'I certainly wasn't ready to love you when Edgar died.'

'You weren't ready to do that even last night.'

'No, last night I was very ready to. In fact, I did so rather beautifully in my opinion,' she told him provocatively.

'But it took you until today to say it.'

'Ah, but today I *know* I love you; yesterday I only thought I did.'

'The power of a good…mmph,' he almost managed to say before she put her hand over his mouth to stop him.

'Don't you dare say that, Maxwell Chilton,' she told him and devilment looked back at her from the darkest, most intriguing male eyes she had ever lost herself in—the only ones she ever looked so deeply

into she lost herself, in fact—and he never could resist a dare.

'Max,' he argued silkily through her splayed fingers, then licked the palm of her hand and she shivered with delight and anticipation and oh, so much
love she actually ached with it. 'And, as I told you
last night, demonstration works so much better than
explanation.'

'Really?' she said and even tried to put some
mockery into it. She must have looked and sounded
unconvincing since he kissed her passionately, in a
stationary carriage in front of half the servants in his
brother's primary country seat, on Lord Elderwood's
finely raked carriage sweep where anyone could have
come along and caught them at it.

'Really,' he said and raised his head long enough
to murmur it before he kissed her again and she forgot where they were and who might be looking.

She was almost certain her legs wouldn't hold
her up so it was as well Max really was the magnificent specimen of mature manhood he had boasted
just now, as that meant he had strength enough for
both of them. He finally jumped down from the carriage, grabbed her in his arms and raced up the lordly
staircase into the nearest bedchamber with her and
slammed the door behind them, before anyone could
question his presence in his brother's primary country seat when Zachary wasn't even here to be ignored
in his own home.

'Really?' she said as soon as she had breath to say

anything at all. 'You really had to do that in front of all your brother's servants?'

'Not all of them. I expect he and Martha took one or two with them when they went to Greygil.'

'And that's supposed to make me feel better?'

'No, it's supposed to make me feel better and you feel loved.'

'Hmm.'

'And wanted,' he said, putting her down so she could meet his urgent kiss with the proper amount of desperation between lovers who hadn't loved one another fully for several hours now. 'Needed, even,' he added huskily, then explored her mouth hungrily at the same time as she felt him fumble with the fastenings of her gown and she had to admire his ambition, even if the method left a lot to be desired.

'I like being needed by you,' she said and unknotted her own laces as he was making such a mess of them in his haste. 'I'm not afraid of you, in any way, my love,' she told him huskily. 'In any way,' she added and tugged him down on to the bed with a long and very passionate kiss and it felt wonderful to be loved in every way there was by him.

'Ah, love,' he managed to murmur between hungry, heated kisses and she heard the shake in his voice as she made it plain even lying under him was part of loving him as far as she was concerned. She didn't feel dominated or afraid, she just felt loved and deliciously open to loving him in every way he was going to teach her for the rest of their lives.

'Yes, that's me: your love,' she said, then kissed him hungrily and hotly back and they were far too busy to think about anything but one another for some time afterwards.

In fact, Zachary's entire staff had eaten their own dinners and begun to wonder about feeding the master's brother and his brother's wife's carefully prepared meal to the pigs before the lovers were finally hungry enough to ring for it to be brought up to whatever bedchamber this was they had appropriated so hastily.

'We are a disgrace, my darling,' Georgia told her husband as she sat up in bed with nothing but a sheet to cover her lack of modesty. 'Huggins will give me notice.'

'Not she, she knows a good mistress when she sees one and so do I.'

'Honestly, Max, I'm your wife!'

'I know,' he said and smiled wolfishly at her, 'and my wife still has six weeks, three days and several hours' worth of her wifely duty to catch up on.'

'Not all at once, surely?'

'You can have the odd hour or two off for good behaviour next week.'

'Thank you.'

'Don't mention it,' he said, so she didn't, she just kissed him again instead.

'I love you, Max. I should always have loved you. I would have done if I knew this was what making love with you felt like. But now I do, I'm never going to stop.'

'When you do manage to get the right words out you do it with your usual flair and determination, Mrs Chilton.'

'I'm so glad you think so, Mr Chilton, and—'

'And there is a time for talking, but this isn't it,' he told her and proved it until there were only six weeks, three days and one less hour left for her to make up on loving her husband immoderately, and immodestly as well.

Epilogue

'Don't worry, you are *not* going to be called Ancaster,' Max told his newly born son nine and a half months later.

Georgia watched him hold the newest Master Chilton so gently that he looked as if he thought the little mite would break if he wasn't very careful with him and she knew babies were really quite tough. 'Or Lochinvar,' she added ruefully.

'Or Charlemagne or Hereward.'

'What are we going to call him, then, Max?'

'I don't know, I had only thought of girls' names before he was born and I really don't think any of them are going to suit him.'

'I wonder about your father's name and my father's for his second name. Papa has never liked it, but it is his name and I want him to be part of his grandson's life.'

'Alexander Horace it is, then. How does that feel, my little man?'

Alexander Horace Chilton burped and looked so surprised at the noise he had made that Georgia chuckled, then wished she hadn't because Alexander Horace was quite a big baby.

'Let's have a girl next time, Max,' she said sleepily, 'they are usually smaller.'

'I hate to think what girls' names his sisters have stored up for future use.'

'Clarabelle-Brilliana was one of the ones they had ready.'

'Best get them another pony, then, they don't know when they're being laughed at.'

'I think Clarabelle-Brilliana Odd-Socks might.'

'Don't make me laugh, I'll wake him up.'

'You really don't know much about babies yet, do you, my love?'

'Well, he's one and Phoebe has only just finished being one, so I should do by now.'

'He's been fed, changed and he's even burped for his papa so of course he's asleep. What else was there left for him to do at his age?'

'Cynic, he was looking at you, probably thinking what a beautiful mother he has.'

'You'll learn, Papa.'

'Oh, I will, my Georgia, and I can't wait,' he said and she believed him and even after giving birth so recently she would not swap a moment of their hectic lives for a quieter one.

'I'm so in love with you, Max.'

'That's not what I heard you yelling a couple of hours ago.'

'I may not always say it, but I always feel it, even at a time like that.'

'You are a paragon among wives, but you talk too much,' he told her with a wicked grin and a kiss full on her mouth to silence her. 'Now go to sleep and dream of me as your wild lover again since that's all we will be able to do for several weeks, if not months.'

'I should never have told you about wanton Georgia and her disgraceful dreams,' she murmured and got ready to do as she was told just this once.

'And if you are very lucky, Alexander Horace Chilton, one day *you* will find a woman who is half as lovely as your mama and almost as much worth dreaming about,' she heard her husband whisper to his new son as he tiptoed out of the room with him.

'And, if she is very lucky indeed, you will love her nearly as much as your father loves me,' she murmured, and fell into an exhausted sleep at last to dream of her wild young lover.

What else was a respectable married woman supposed to do when that was all they could do for the next few weeks? Max was so worth dreaming about she might as well get on and enjoy another one while she had the chance.

* * * * *